THE WAY TO A KILLER'S HEART 2

NEICY P.

The Way to A Killer's Heart 2

Copyright by @ Neicy P.

Published by: Shan Presents

www.shanpresents.com

All rights reserved.

This book is a work of fiction. Names, characters, places, and incidents either are the product of the author's imagination or are used fictitiously and are not to be construed as real. Any resemblance to actual persons, living or dead, business establishments, events, or locales, is entirely coincidental.

No part of this book may be used or reproduced in any manner whatsoever without the prior written consent of the publisher and author, except in the case of brief quotations embodied in critical articles and reviews.

SUBSCRIBE

Text Shan to 22828 to stay up to date with new releases, sneak peeks, contest, and more...

WANT TO BE A PART OF SHAN PRESENTS?

To submit your manuscript to Shan Presents, please send the first three chapters and synopsis to submissions@shanpresents.com

PROLOGUE

JOEL

I was sitting at the bus stop, waiting on my Momma to pick me up. She was usually standing here before my bus arrived. I knew my way home. She just didn't feel comfortable with me walking home alone. If she only knew what my dad had been teaching me when I went over there for the summer. And if it wasn't him, my brothers were banging me up for fun. I was pretty tough for a twelve-year-old girl.

I looked down the street to see if she was coming. Our house was at the other end of the corner. I looked down at my watch, to check the time. *3:30pm.*

"Momma is going to be so mad at me." I said and began walking towards my house. School was alright today. I aced my Calculus test with ease. All of the other kids tried to copy off my paper, but I didn't let them. It was tough being the smartest kid in the 9th grade. I was hoping that they would skip me again, so that I could go to college and train more with my Parrain. He pushed me more and didn't hold back. That was something that I needed if I was going to work in the family business.

NEICY P.

I reached my house and saw our neighbors sitting on the front porch. Mr. and Mrs. Perry. Mr. Perry didn't talk too much, but it looked like he had a lot to say. When he did, Mrs. Perry would talk for him. The thing was, with Mrs. Perry, she didn't know when to stop talking. I knew that she would tell Momma if I didn't speak and I was going to get in trouble for that. I passed them up and walked into the gate. I pulled my key out and looked over at them.

"Hi Mr. and Mrs. Perry." I said.

"Hey there, Joel. How was school today Precious?" She smiled and said.

"It was ok." I told her quickly. She kept talking and talking. I reached the door with my key but stopped when Mr. Perry started talking.

"Joel your uncles came by. They wanted to surprise your Mom and they are waiting for your Dad." I took a step back and looked over at him. He nodded his head and grabbed Mrs. Perry's hand. "Come on Jasmine, our shows are about to come on." He told her.

"Oh, they sho is. Bye, Ms. Joel. Tell your mother that I said to call me when y'all family leaves." She said and walked inside the house. Mr. Perry stared at me and smiled. I didn't know what that was about. But, what I did know was that there weren't any uncles. My mother was the only child and my father's brothers died before I was born.

I jumped over the railing and went through the side gate. I didn't know who or how many was in the house. The only thing that bothered me, was that they were in there with my Momma. We lived in a two-bedroom home. Our bedrooms were on the left and everything else was on the right. I pulled an old milk carton crate from under the house and pushed it near the window. I eased up and looked towards the door first. There was no one there. I stepped down and pushed the crate to the next window. I heard voices coming from our kitchen.

I stepped up on it and looked through the window. My mother was tied up in one of our dining room chairs with two men in front of her and one standing behind her. The one that was behind my mom was black, medium built with cornrows in his head. The other two were black as well, but they were bigger than the other guy, taller even. One of them was wearing a black shirt, the other was wearing a red one.

"What time does your daughter get home, Lady?" The one behind her asked.

My mother shook her head before saying, "I don't know. She's into all type of after-school activities. She probably won't be back until after five." She said with tears in her eyes. I felt the rage building up and taking over my body.

"What do you want to do now, Boss?" Black shirt said.

"We are going to wait, 'til Mack's little bitch get here and when she does, she will suffer the same faith as her mother." He laughed and grabbed my mother's breast roughly. She jerked away from him and spat in his face. Cornrows raised his hand and punched my mother in the face. "Since you gotta be a bitch about it, we can start on you now." He told her and nodded to red shirt.

Red shirt picked her up and carried her to the family room. My mother started screaming and scratching at the guy. She must have got him good, because he dropped her and called her a bitch. Momma ran to the window that I was looking through. She saw my face and turned her back towards me. She held her hand up and surrendered.

"Ok. Ok. Ok. I'll do whatever you want. Just, please. Leave my baby girl alone. She doesn't have anything to do with this." She begged.

Red shirt walked up to Momma and grabbed her by her hair. He slapped and dragged her to the family room. I stepped down off the crate and closed my eyes. Kymani and Kymel told me about this feeling. My eyes closed, and my blood began to boil. I could feel my soul floating out of my body. Emotions, feelings, or anything else that made me the sweet little girl before, were gone. I opened my eyes and saw the world through a new set of eyes.

I took a deep breath and walked towards the other side of my house. They were distracted by what they were trying to do to my mom. I climbed the gate and opened my bedroom window. I peeked in to be cautious, then leaped through. I moved quietly to my closet and went to the top shelf where I hid my special knives. Kymani saw how well I handled myself with them and thought that these were good enough for my small hands. I opened the box and pulled out my gold M48 Cyclone Blades. They weren't small, but I was able to handle them. I walked out the room and heard my mother screaming. I got to the door and measured how far the voices were. *3ft for one and 6ft for the other.* I stood close to the wall and took even breaths. *Slow and easy, El.*

I stepped out and threw the blade with enough pressure to land where I wanted it. I didn't wait for it to hit its target because the other was coming towards me. I dodged his hands and stabbed him in his thigh. I twisted the blade and pulled it out. My other blade was hanging out of the throat of the one in the black shirt. The man in the red shirt was screaming like a girl. I grabbed him by his hair and stuck the blade under his chin. I saw my blade through his opened mouth. My eyes stayed on his. I smirked and watched the life he thought was good, vanish from his eyes.

The door to the family room opened. Cornrows came running out there with his pants down and a gun in his hand. I grabbed my blade and waited for him to make the first move. He looked over at his two dead buddies on the floor.

"What the hell?" He said. He looked at me with bewildered eyes. "You are just like them." He told me and raised his gun. I smirked at him right before I dodged the first bullet. He moved the gun to the right and I went left, he moved left, and I moved right. I got to him just in time to slice the wrist that was holding the gun. It dropped in my open hand and I shot him in both of his knees.

"AHHH," he screamed. It was too bad for him that I wasn't done. I stood over him and started stabbing him wildly. I wasn't aiming for any specific spot. If there were holes in his body, I was satisfied. I heard my mother's footsteps coming towards me. I couldn't look up at her because I didn't want to stop. I stabbed and stabbed until I was tired. There was blood everywhere. I was drenched in it. I took deep breaths in and out. I was trying to calm down and regain back some type of sanity.

I couldn't.

I was high off the kills.

I enjoyed it too much and wanted more of it. Something that I had never felt came over me. It was an indescribable feeling that had my head dropping back. I moaned out, like I just ate some warm chocolate cookies.

I looked up at my mom and it looked like she was beaten more in the bedroom. Her mouth was busted, and her eye was swollen. But that didn't hide her expression. She was.... scared of me. There was nothing that I could say or do to make her feel better. I was what I was, and Momma had to get used to it. It was in my blood.

The front door began to rattle like someone was trying to get in. I pulled the blade out of Cornrows and threw it at the door, just when it opened. I rolled over to the other body and retrieved my blade from his throat. I jumped back in front of my mother and squatted. I was ready for whoever thought that they were going to hurt Momma again.

A tall, dark skin man walked through the door with a calm expression. I waited still. Two other men walked through the door with smiles on their face. "Wow Joel. Mi feel that kill an it feel gud." Kymani said. I kept my eyes on the first man that walked in. He took a step towards me and I sneered at him. He stopped and stared back.

"Princess yuh kno who stand inna front eff yuh." He asked. I continued staring with the blade held tightly in my hand. He tilted his head and I tilted mine. I raised my eyebrow at him. He closed his eyes and his facial expressions changed. His eyes went black and he dared me to challenge him. "It nuh wah yuh wa dawta." He told me.

Something inside me wanted to back down and run into this man's arms, but I couldn't. I hated and loved him for some reason. I didn't agree with a lot of things that he has done. I wanted to tell him in so many ways why I had this type of anger towards him. But, I couldn't look vulnerable to them. Kymel began to walk towards my right. His eyes were like the other man. Kymani shifted and began to walk to my left. I saw all of this but kept my eyes on him. I knew what their plans were. I had to remain focused. Kymani started making tapping sounds with his lighter. They were getting closer, but they knew not to get within 5ft of me or they were going to get hurt.

"Joel!" Momma yelled out. In that second, the man grabbed the blade out of the wall and threw it at me. I deflected it with the other blade. It went towards Kymel. Kymani grabbed my mother and pulled her back. I swung my blade at him and missed. Pain shot up my arm, when a big hand wrapped around my wrist. I dropped the blade and started swinging. He caught my fist, but not the kick to his shin. It did the right amount of damage that I needed to hit him in his throat. Kymani came over and grabbed my arm. I swung with the other. He blocked it and hit my pressure point in the arm that he held. That didn't stop me.

I kicked him in the knee and rolled on his back when he bent. When I was on the other side of him, I kicked him in the butt towards the other man. Kymel tried to grab my other arm. I spun underneath his arm. He swung back around right in time for my fist to connect in that special spot. My special spot. The other man and Kymani recovered and came for me again. I stepped on the handle of the gun and kicked it up. I caught it and aimed it at the two.

The other man stared over at me. Kymani stood next to him as Kymel struggled to breathe. My aim was perfect. The only thing that I had to do was to pull the trigger. Something was telling me that this was wrong. *Not Kymel.* I thought. I looked over at him and he was pleading for me to remember why not him. I glanced back at the other two men and knew why when I saw the look in their eyes. They were now staring at me with love. I felt my soul coming back into my body, and I was dropping from that high. The other man looked familiar now. He looked like... my father. I let out a deep breath and dropped the gun. My Poppa smiled and held his arms out to me. I went into them and squeezed him tightly. "Breathe Kymel. Just breathe." I said out loud. Kymel took in a deep breath and started coughing.

"Rajae teach yuh di special spot." My Poppa asked.

"Yeah. He told me that the boys weren't ready for it." I replied tiredly. Kymani laughed and ruffled my hair. Kymel got off the floor and stood in front of us.

"Yuh fast Joel. Mi a guh haffi watch yuh. Mi nuh way uh taking my spot." He said with a grunt.

"She ain't taking shit. What the hell Callum? I told you not to train my daughter to do this. She doesn't need to be in your world." Momma said. I knew that I scared the heck out of her. She had to understand that it was because of my training that we lived. Poppa looked over to her and shook his head. He kissed my head and went to her.

"She is our daughter, Cassidy." He said with no accent. He was training us to adapt to our surroundings. But sometimes when they got real mad or was around family, they couldn't control their native tongue. "I told you in the beginning that they were going to find out about her. If you wanted her to stay here with you, she was going to have to learn how to defend herself. I wasn't going to leave our child stranded." He told her. She shook her head to say something else, but he stopped her. "This won't be the last time Cassidy. There will be more, and they will be more experienced than these clowns. Joel will come stay with me and my family. I will take care of her." Poppa told her.

I loved my brothers and my Poppa. But there was no way that I was leaving my Momma. She wasn't trained and didn't know anything about the life that my Poppa lived. If someone comes for her and I am not here, I will lose it and there would be nothing to bring me back. "Mi wa stay Poppa." I whispered. He looked over at me with a frown. Not because of what I said, but because I had interfered in an adult conversation. He didn't play that at all. I lowered my head to show him respect. He walked over to me and lifted my head up by my chin.

"Neva again." He demanded. I maintained eye contact and apologized with my eyes. He went back to Momma and she was shaking her head.

"You are not taking my baby, Callum. She is all that I have." Momma said with her trembling lips. Poppa sighed and looked back at me. He knew how much I loved my Momma. If he took me away, I was going to do more than act out. He knew it too, because when I looked back at him, he was smiling.

"Kymani, you will stay the first four months. If we get orders out here, I'll send them to you. But you have to work around your sister's and Cassidy's schedule," Poppa told him.

Kymani smiled and came to pick me up in a hug. "That's cool with me Poppa. I'll be happy to spend some time with my little sister." Kymel looked like he was pouting. Poppa told him that he had the four months after the summer break. I looked over at Momma to see if she was cool with that. She nodded her head in relief.

"Now that, that is over. Let's go and get your face fixed up." He told her and led her to the bathroom. Before they cleared the room, I had to ask something that was bothering me. "Poppa, how did you know that we needed you?"

He turned with a smirk on my face. "I knew you didn't need me. I just wanted to be here when you kill them. Malcolm told me that men were passing by when you were at school. He thought that it was something and called me." He said and continued into the bathroom.

"Who is Malcolm?" I asked.

"Malcolm is your neighbor, Mr. Perry." Kymel said walking into the kitchen. I was shocked. Mr. Perry knew my Poppa. I wanted to ask more but got instantly tired. I put my head on my big brother's shoulder and went to sleep. And to be honest, it was the best sleep ever. I guess I really was born to do this.

GAGE

I was standing in front of the group of men that sent assassins to kill my children. Rage didn't describe what I was feeling at that time. I wanted heads to roll and afterwards, I wanted to bathe in their blood. I haven't felt like this in a while. I looked over at each of them and didn't feel no remorse for what was about to happen. Jason looked angry as usual. But who didn't give a fuck, was me. I wasn't the woman he knew back then. I was different. I was much more lethal because I had something to live and die for.

"You want us to believe that this bitch is Gage." Greg Sr. said. "Now, this is a new low for you, Callum. Bringing little girls to the men's table." My father didn't respond. My brothers didn't either. I had been called a bitch before by many. This wasn't any different. I continued staring into the eyes of the man that broke my heart and almost broke me. Thanks to Tyja and my children, I hadn't been treading the waters, until my brother called me and told me that a couple of men came after my babies.

I didn't play behind them. No fucking way. I knew that they could handle themselves if the time came. When I heard that they were in danger behind Joseph's mess, I was more than happy to come back and introduce myself as Gage. The one that they all feared. I held my machete up towards Greg Sr. and spoke as calmly as possible.

"Yuh need an example." Poppa took the chair and spun it in my direction. Shadow and Reap took a step back to get a better view. They hadn't seen me in action in a while.

Greg Sr. nodded to his right-hand man, Lenny. He smiled and began removing his guns from his holsters. "You really trying to prove a point, aren't you?" Lenny asked him. The rest of his men chuckled behind them.

"Get this shit over with, so that we can take care of the rest of these fools." Greg Sr. told him with a wave of his hand.

I hated arrogant muthafuckers like that. Always underestimating the women. What they didn't know, was that I was the most dangerous person in that room. And Greg Sr. just sent his best man in those waters, without testing it. Lenny was finally ready to die after removing his items that he won't be retrieving. He started walking towards me. I didn't wait. Poppa said it best in the beginning when he said that we had better things to do.

I walked to meet him halfway. I tossed my machete over to Shadow and dodged Lenny's meaty fist right before he swung at my face. I reached under his arm and took out his throat with one move. Greg Sr.'s men gasped and pulled out their guns. I knew that they weren't going to shoot. My Parrain had targets on everyone here, including the Davis family.

When he found out what happened, he didn't waste time coming out of retirement. Poppa and Parrain didn't want to miss this. Even if they didn't get to kill anyone. Lenny was on his knees gurgling on his own blood. I dropped my head back and felt that exhilarated feeling I always felt after every kill. My brothers and I were so close that they felt the kill too. They told me that it felt like having an orgasm. Poppa cleared his throat a little to shake off his feeling. I looked back over at Greg Sr. and smirked at him. I strolled over to him and placed Lenny's throat in his lap. I grabbed the back of his shirt and wiped the blood of Lenny on it. Since it was his fault that he died, he should be the one to wear it.

I walked back over to Shadow and he shook his head. "Mi nuh feel dat inna while." He said more relaxed than before.

"Get ready, cuz yuh bout to feel it nuff more." I told him. Reaper smiled and waited until I gave them the ok.

"Wait, this must be a misunderstanding. We would never go after any of you." Sean, Sr.

"No nuh wi. But mi pickney. Yuh come afta dem." I whispered.

"What fucking children?" I heard Jason ask. He wasn't my main concern right now. I had to finish this job, or I was going to finish up with him and his brothers. I maintained eye contact with him without answering his questions. JJ stood up with Jason and Joseph. He stared at me with his mouth opened. I never had anything against Joseph. He always looked out for Jason when he went over to the other side or when Joseph was using him. "Are you fucking serious right now? You had Jason baby?" He asked.

"Babies," Poppa corrected. He was still tapping on his phone. The children showed him some type of game that could keep him calm when he got pissed. I tried the Dancing Lines game but got pissed when I didn't make it to the end.

"What do you mean, babies?" Jason asked him. Poppa looked over at Jason and shook his head. None of them wanted to talk to him after what he had done to me. I had to threaten all three of them. I felt that Jason was my problem. If anyone was going to deal with him, it was going to be me.

"Gage had babies for Jason." Derrick asked. Poppa looked up at him with a smile on his face. You could see that he was getting tired of repeating the same shit over and over again. He was relieved that he figured it out, so they would know why we were here. And why they were going to be killed.

"How were we supposed to know about the children? We only sent them after Jordan's children." Sean Sr. said. He wasn't with this from the beginning. He let the rest of the men talk him into it.

David Sr. sat back without a worry in the world. He thought that the assassins they ordered was going to show up. What he didn't know was that they were already dead. That was our first stop. We were there to finish off the job. Well, I was there to finish things off. Shadow and Reap was supposed to kill off their guards. "I still don't see what this had to do with you, Callum. We heard that you weren't that close to your employees. Why come all the way out here for someone that works for you?" David Sr. said.

Poppa leaned forward and spoke in perfect English. "Like I told y'all punk asses before. I almost felt the pain that you were talking about. When my sons called and told me that someone sent assassins for my grandchildren, I lost it. We got the information from the men and that led us to you." He responded.

Everybody's faces dropped at that point. Poppa just told them who he was and what we were to him. So that meant that he was giving me the ok to kill everybody in that room. Reaper started laughing and walked closer to me.

"Yuh ready sista." He whispered in my ear.

"Wait! Wait! This has to be some type of mistake." Derrick Sr. screamed.

The Stand guards placed their hands on their weapons. Some had their weapons out still, waiting for their bosses to give them the order to start shooting. I felt the familiar tingling in my fingers. Jason stood still and placed his hands on his brother's shoulder.

"Sit and don't move." Jason told them. He kept his eyes on me and waited for what was about to happen.

I looked over to Shadow and nodded my head. Before the first shot rang out, the room went dark. I leaped over Poppa and ran on the table, severing heads of my enemies. I had seen flashes of guns going off by the guards. I avoided all the bullets and deflected some that were headed to the Davis crew. Men screamed out in pain, while the music and the tapping sound on Poppa's phone remained. When I reached the end of the table, the lights were back on and my brothers were standing next to me, covered in blood.

"Yass!" I moaned out.

Shadow and Reap were moving their heads from side to side. They were trying to escape the feeling that had taken over their bodies. That was why killing and torturing muthafuckers became addictive to us. We were able to release built-up energy and put our fucked-up minds to rest.

"Holy shit." Tank whispered.

I glanced back and saw the men standing. Jason stared at me with curious eyes. Eyes that I had seen in many of the lives I had taken. He wanted to know if he could take me. I smirked at him and shook my head. Shadow turned towards them and had one thing on his mind. He was ready to clean house. I placed my hand on his chest and stopped him. He looked back at me with soulless eyes. Having overprotective brothers that knew how to torment and kill people, made life hard for me. Imagine the boyfriends that had to meet them or my father. If they couldn't withstand their stare, they were deemed unworthy to be in my presence.

Reap took a step forward and I stopped him with a glare. "Let's go." I told him. He mean-mugged me and looked over to Poppa. Poppa's eyes stared into my own. I told him in many ways that I didn't want this to happen without reason.

"Yuh sure baby."

"Yes, Poppa, mi sure." I whispered. He nodded his head and stood from his chair. He looked over at Jason and the rest of the men.

"Reap. Shadow. Let yuh sista handle this." He told them and walked off towards the exit. Reap scoffed and walked behind them. Shadow didn't want to. He was ready to kill them all. I grabbed his face and directed his attention to me.

"They are waiting." I told him. His face changed from the killer to the loving uncle. He nodded and grabbed my hand. I walked out of the warehouse without a backwards glance.

We got outside, and I saw Parrain sitting in his brand-new Cadillac waiting on Poppa. I rode with Reap and Shadow in a black Ford-150 King Ranch. That was one of the things I admired the most about my family. We had the money to ball out, but that wasn't something we cared about. We wanted to stay under the radar as much as possible. We were able to afford an island of our own if we wanted it, but we all remained in the same home, under Poppa's roof.

Reap reached the car and waited for us. The warehouse door burst open with a pissed off Jason running towards me. Reap stood up straighter and Parrain stepped out of the car. Shadow squeezed my hand.

"Yuh wa mi to tek him out." He asked. I squeezed his hand back, tighter.

"Eff yuh touch him bredda, yuh wi regret it. Mi wi tek care of dis." I told him.

I handed him my machete and motioned for him to keep walking. I turned around just in time to duck from Jason's first attack. His brothers and cousin stood and watched while Jason missed every attempt to lay my ass out. He didn't have a chance. When he looked like he had me, I dodged him each time. His rage was fueling him on, and that was what made him careless. I could have taken him out right before he swung on me the first time.

When he saw that he couldn't touch me, he pulled out a knife. He swung it and it caught the tip of my hair, chopping off a couple inches of it. He came down with the knife and it slice open my leather jacket. I felt Shadow and Reap coming closer. I didn't want them to intervene, so I grabbed Jason's wrist when he swung. I held onto it with my left hand and punched his pressure point with my right. It had him dropping the knife, but it put my back towards him. Jason wrapped his other arm around my neck and squeezed tightly.

My brothers came forward. Parrain and Poppa stayed back and watched. They knew that I could get out of that hold. They were surprised that I would be so careless to put my back towards him. I knew why, and I wasn't planning on sharing it with no one. Jason's mouth was close to my ear. I knew he wanted to kill me after what he found out in that room.

"You lied to me. You told me that I could trust you. I let you in my home. My family. And in my heart. You fucking played me for what, to get close and kill my family. Me." He spat out. I grabbed the arm that was around my neck, as he continued with his rant. "I fucking loved you. You kept my children from me and thought that I would let you walk out this bitch without saying shit." He said with hate. Hate that he didn't have the right to have. When I went to Lilly's doctor's appointment, Tyja's phone alerted that her menstrual cycle was two days away. It was sad how busy her life was that she had to make that stupid alert. She told us that we had to stop at Walgreens to get her some tampons. I told her that I had some at my house and the thought of my own cycle came to me. I haven't had one since me and Jason hooked up. I told the girls and Lily asked the doctor if I could take a pregnancy test. I wasn't against being pregnant; I just wasn't ready for a baby right now.

When the test came out positive, all sorts of feelings rushed me. One that surprised me was being happy. I felt that Jason would have me and the baby to keep him from going over. I couldn't wait to tell him and Ma-Ma the good news. We got to Ma-Ma's house and found out that someone killed Pops. I was pissed that they had let him out by himself knowing that he was a target. I heard Joseph telling Jason that it was his fault that Pops was killed. The look that overcame his face was of hate and directed towards me.

When Joseph threatened me, it was fine. That was something that I could handle, but not from Jason. That shit pushed me over and had me ready to take him out. Thank God Tyja and Lilly reminded me of my bundle of joy that I was carrying. That alone had me walking out of the door.

His arm tightening brought me out of my daydream. He just didn't know that his arm around my neck was four-play. I was turned on more than I was afraid. My heartbeat spiked up in anticipation for a good fuck afterwards, then something he said stopped all the throbbing that was goin on between my legs. *I fucking loved you.* Hearing that shit, pissed me off. I waited for him to tell me those words when we were together and he said it now, regrettable. I hit the other pressure point in his other wrist and bucked my head back, hitting him in the nose. I pushed out of his arms and hit the special spot that had him dropping to his knees.

I leaned over him and stared into his eyes. "You loved me." I said sarcastically. "You couldn't have loved me enough to trust that I was going to help you get through whatever pain that you were going through. You trusted a fucking brother that used you for his own personal gain over a woman that showed you a side of yourself that you didn't know existed." I got closer to his face and continued. "Keep you and your family bullshit off my doorstep. Or I'll unleash a promising death to you all." I stood up straight and turned my back towards him this time knowing that his ass wasn't going to attack again.

I heard his family yelling out his name as his breathing became shallow. My brothers turned and walked towards the car. I stopped when I heard JJ calling out to me. I turned, and he was running towards me with a gun pointed in my direction. "I don't give a fuck who you are, but if my brother dies, so do you." He said. Shadow took out his gun and was going to shot without warning. I held my hand up and stopped him.

"There is nothing wrong with your brother Jordan." I looked over at Jason and it looked like he was about to take his last breath. "All he has to do is breathe." I said and watched him take in a deep breath. JJ backed up with the gun still on me. He looked down at Jason's bloody face and saw that he was breathing ok.

I walked back to the truck and got in the back seat. The Davis crew watched as we pulled off from their meeting. I pulled out my phone and looked down at the picture of my babies. Mason and Madison. They had their father's eyes and both of our attitude. I couldn't wait to see my babies again. My face time ring began to go off. Hazel's eyes were the first thing I saw, and I was back into Mommy mode.

"Hey Mommy, are you finish yet?" Madison spoke. My daughter had the most beautiful, smooth caramel complexion and a round face with chubby cheeks. Baby girl's thick eyelashes fanned over her hazel eyes. Her curly hair was up in two ponytails and her lips were red from whatever she was eating.

"Yes baby, Mommy is on her way. Along with Uncle Mel and Uncle Mani." I told her.

She let out a deep breath before asking another question. "Is Daddy coming with you this time?" I smiled and shook my head.

"He is not ready, Pretty. It will be soon though. Very soon. Do you believe me?" I asked her. She nodded her head without hesitation. I

THE WAY TO A KILLER'S HEART 2

looked over her shoulder for Mason. I knew if she was up, so was he. He always went to sleep after her. Mason was already overprotective of his sister and me.

"He is sitting right here watching the video that Uncle Mel sent him." Madison responded knowing my next question.

"What video did you send to Mason, Mel?" I asked him.

"The one that Pops recorded in the warehouse." Kymel responded.

"Ugh, are you two serious? Why would y'all send him that?" I asked.

"He wanted to see his father, Sis. What you wanted us to tell him, no?" He said and turned around.

Mason was asking for his father more and more. I knew that my brothers weren't going to be able to replace Jason, but I was hoping that they could answer any questions that Mason had that I couldn't answer. But, the real question could only be answered by me.

Ma-Ma and Tee Glen came by often to check on us. She sometimes brought Lily and JoJo with her. Lily told JoJo not to tell his father or his uncles about his cousins. We told him that it was a secret and that we wanted to surprise them. Ma-Ma knew that she was taking a chance every time that she visited.

"I just don't want to miss my other grandbabies growing up. If Jason don't have the mindset to be there for his children as a father, then I will be here as their grandmother." She told me. I was more than happy to have them here. She brought pictures of Jason when he was small and told them stories about him growing up. Mason and Madison retold the stories to each other at bedtime.

"Madison, can you please put Mason on the phone?" I asked her. She nodded and placed the phone in front of Mason. He was focused on the video that was replaying on his phone. He paused it and stared.

"Daddy," he whispered. I smiled at the sentiment. He loved this man with all his flaws.

"Mason," I called out.

"I look just like him, Momma." He said to me with admiration.

"I know baby." I responded. He kept his eyes on the phone.

"Momma, I need to see him."

"You will baby. I will talk to your Grandma and see if we can set something up." I promised him. He looked up at the response and smiled with those deep dimples.

"Thank you, Mommy. You are the best." He said. He stretched out in his bed and continued staring at his father. Madison turned the phone back to herself and blew me a kiss.

"I am going to sleep now. Can you please come to our room when you get home? I miss you so much." She told me. I blew a kiss back at her.

"I miss you too, my Pretty. I will see you both soon." I told her and hung up the phone.

JASON

J was sitting on the ground outside the warehouse. I couldn't believe what I found out. Joel was Gage and she had my children. I was in love with someone more dangerous than I was. That was why she completed me. She understood my crazy because she dealt with it in herself and in her brothers. I took in a deep breath and stood to my feet with Jo and Tank's help.

"We gotta get out of here." Jo said.

JJ pulled up in front of us and pushed the passenger door open. Jo helped me in the car and got in the back seat with Tank. JJ pulled off and jumped on the interstate.

"Where are we going?" JJ asked.

"Home," Jo replied. I leaned my head back on the seat and closed my eyes. I knew that they had questions and wanted to talk about what happened. They all were waiting on me to start it up. I opened my eyes and saw that JJ was glancing over at me. I sighed and gave him permission to start.

"Talk JJ."

"Look, I know that you are feeling some type of way with Joel being Gage, but man. Joel is Gage. Like real life, she is a fucking assassin. Not just any assassin. The coldest muthafucker in the game right now." JJ spoke.

"Calm the fuck down, nigga." Tank yelled. "She ain't that cold." He said unsure.

"Fuck that. She almost took Jason out with one punch. You can't tell me that, that wasn't some cold shit." JJ responded back while turning on Ma's street. He looked over at me again with an unusual look. "You have kids, bruh. A set of twins. They are how old, you think?"

I sat their quietly and didn't answer him. I didn't know the age of my children or if they were boys or girls. That shit had me ready to punch a hole in the nearest wall. My mind was racing at that moment. I couldn't believe that I was a father, to two kids. I didn't know what type of game Joel was playing, but I wasn't for it. JJ pulled into the gate and stopped in front of the house. I jumped out before anyone else. Ma was in the family room with Tee Glen and Lily.

"What the hell happened to your face, boy?" Tee Glen asked. Tank shook his head and sat next to her on the couch. "Joel happened to him." He replied.

"Yeah, better known as Gage." Jo answered as well. I looked over to Ma and didn't see the surprised expression that I thought that we were going to see. I saw a woman that was relieved that the secret was out. I looked over at the rest of the women and they looked the same. Guilty. Jo looked at Lily the same way. "I know you are not about to tell us that you knew this already." He told her.

She looked back at him with her eyebrows bunched up. "And if I did." She replied.

Jo shook his head and looked like he wanted to choke her ass out. I walked over to where Ma was sitting and stood over her. She stared back at me with love in her eyes. At that moment, I didn't need it. I needed the truth. I was still dizzy from the headbang that Joel gave me. I knew that whatever Ma was about to tell me, was going to have me passing out. I hadn't been talking to her like I used to, and I knew that it was long overdue.

"Tell me." I asked her.

She leaned forward and motioned me to bend down. I looked down at her and shook my head no. She smirked up at me and stood to her feet. She walked past me and walked to the bar in the room.

"When we were on our way from the doctor's appointment, Joel pushed me to the floor of the car. When I looked up, she was shooting at the men in the car. The way she handled that gun, was of a skillful killer. I knew that she was someone dangerous. She caught me looking at her, and I saw the same thing I used to see in your eyes when you went all black and gone. It was different with her, though. Joel was darker and seemed more threatening. The shock on my face made her jump back into that sweet Joel and she started helping JJ out with his wound. Once I got her alone, I brought up what I saw in her pretty eyes. Joel smiled and began telling me who she was."

"That she was here to kill us." I interrupted.

"No, that she was here to get away from it all. Joel was here because she was thinking of retiring. The night when Curtis called and told you that he was sending someone over to her house to take her. She got a text from her contact saying that they were men surrounding her house. She went home and took care of them, before the call was received. She heard that Curtis was the one that sent those men after her and us, she called in and told them to reactivate Gage. She went and killed Curtis and everyone that he was affiliated with and came back to live a happy life with you. I told your father as well. He knew who she was the first day she came to the house."

Ma poured a drink in three glasses. She picked them up and gave one to JJ, Jordan, and then handed the last one to me. "She was never here to kill you or the family. Joel was a woman, who fell in love with a man. That became another reason to get out of that business." Ma grabbed my jaw with one hand and a smile appeared on her face. "You became her light Jason. A man that had all the demons in his closet, became something positive to a woman that became nightmares to many." Ma told me.

I threw the glass of liquor to the wall of the house. "I don't want to hear that shit, Ma. She fucking lied to me. Joel had time to tell me who she was." I yelled. The fact that Pops knew and didn't tell us had me feeling some type of way.

"And then what. You would have thought that she was trying to kill you. That is what you were thinking. All of you were thinking the same thing." Lily intervened. I looked over at her and she stared back at me, boldly.

"She fucking lied." I yelled out again.

"Boy get over it. She lied. Oh, fucking well. She wasn't out here trying to kill you and your greedy ass brother. She let you both live after y'all threatened her. The girl loved you and she loves you still. What woman do you know gives birth to two children of a man she didn't love?" Tee Glean said. I turned to look at her, surprised.

"Many," JJ said.

"Joel ain't many. You could see that she got her head on her shoulder. She is a good woman." She said.

Tank sat up to get a better angle of his mother. "Mom, you knew about the children." He asked her.

She let out a sigh and stared up at me. I looked over to Ma and she mirrored the same expression as Tee Glen.

"You knew." I whispered with my blood boiling. JJ came to stand next to me and waited for Ma to answer. Ma glanced at the both of us and nodded her head.

"After Joel left, Lily told me about the pregnancy. I called Joel's phone and she didn't answer me for two months. I finally got through when Tyja called me and told me that Joel was having trouble carrying the twins. The doctor put her on bed rest and told her to stay away from stress. So, she went to Florida, where her brothers and father were, to relax. I went to the house and was greeted with love as always from Callum's boys. I saw Joel sitting in the bed reading some of those books that Lily gave her when she was here with us. I sat with her and we talked about the babies and what she was to expect for the next months. I started going out there once a month with your Tee Glen and then with Lily. The day you guys wanted to celebrate your father's birthday, I couldn't because Joel was giving birth to your son and daughter." She said with a smile.

But, I was far from happy. "You knew all this shit about Joel and didn't bother telling me. It looked like you have more loyalty to that lying bitch then you have to me. Your own son." I said, heatedly.

"Loyalty. Loyalty!" Ma stood and got in my face. "Loyalty is stepping in for your children when you couldn't. Loyalty is being there for them and making sure that they knew who you are, when they see you. Loyalty is having your back and making sure you're safe, even when you are out there being careless with your life. Loyalty is something I instilled in you, since birth. I made you boy. Everything about you is either me or your father. So, check yourself before you spit out some bullshit about loyalty." She told me in a murderous tone.

"Speak that shit Joyce. His punk ass forgot that we ain't new to this shit." Tee Glen said, standing behind Ma's back.

Ma took a step back and grilled me some more. "And if I ever hear you call Joel a bitch again, you will regret it." She said and walked out of the room with Tee Glen and Lily following. JJ was still standing next to me, staring off at Ma.

"I thought that she was about to go get Matilda. You had Ma spitting and shit." He told me. I wasn't in the mood for none of that shit. I was ready to go home, get a nut, or body someone.

"Man, what are we going to do? The Elites murdered the Stand in front of us. You know they are going to think that Jo finally came up with a plan to kill them off. That is another war that we are going to have to fight." Tank said.

"Let them think whatever. Clearly, the Stand called us out there to kill us. They got dealt with and that is that. Nobody ain't gon' tell or ask us shit about it." Jo spoke.

"For real, nigga. They not gon' say shit to us, bro. Jason got these fools shook." JJ replied.

Before Pops passed, Joel kept me level-headed. She showed me how I could have been different. Oh, but I was a straight savage now. I got into some heavy torturing shit that had everyone calling for my services. I was walking around without a conscience and no leash. I didn't communicate with my fam like I used to. If it wasn't about business, I didn't want to hear about it. I wasn't attending family dinners, birthdays, or any other holiday that they had celebrated. I stayed to myself. I looked at JJ and mumbled something under my breath. I knew it pissed Jo and Tank off when I did that shit.

"Aight, bruh. Just call me when you get up." JJ replied. I tried to lift my hand to dap him off, but the shit was still hurting from Joel's attack. I turned and walked out the house with Jo and Tank calling after me. I ignored them. I got into my black 2017 Mustang Coupe and peeled out of the gate. I needed to get away from them before I did something that I would have regretted.

I was pissed off more at myself, than at the others. I knew Joel was different from the other women. The way she stood up to Joseph, and the way she calmed me down was proof. I looked past all of that and continued the relationship. I needed it to be real and that was how she got into my heart. The same way I let Mya or whatever her name was, slip through as well. Mya was my kill and she knew that. That was why she gifted me with her head. I was grateful, but I wanted her blood on my hands.

I pulled up to my new condo in the city. I didn't go back to the home that me and Joel shared. I didn't want to relive the memories of us and everything that we had been through. The home that she used to stay in was right next to the interstate. I went out of my way to avoid seeing her house. That was another reason why I didn't go to my parents' home a lot. She left her things in my room. Her perfume, soap, brush, and clothes were there. I didn't want to move them because deep down, I needed them there. As much as I didn't want to remember her, I still needed it to be the proof of something.

I bought a building with four floors. Each floor had two condos on them. The fourth floor was where my condo was. I opened my car door and entered the building. There was an older black woman that worked the front desk. She never spoke to me and that was the way I liked it. I didn't do small talk anymore. It never led me anywhere. I pressed the up button on my private elevator and waited. A text message came through my phone just when the door opened. I pulled out my phone and saw that it was Sierra.

Sierra was a chick that I was fucking for a couple of years now.

THE WAY TO A KILLER'S HEART 2

Her father was a gun boss on the west side. I met her three years ago at JJ's club. Sierra and her friends were having a party there, and JJ asked me to pick up some shit for him. She was in the VIP section dancing to some woman talking about, *fuck em then I get some money.* The way her body was moving had me bricked up. I went in their VIP section, grabbed her hips, and pulled her body to mine. I leaned in and whispered in her ear. "Meet me downstairs in five minutes."

Sierra removed my hands and stepped forward. She turned around and was ready to go in on me, like I was some random. Once she saw my face, her mouth formed into a sexy smile. Baby girl was gorgeous. She was chocolate with deep brown eyes. She had hips, thighs, titties, and ass. I knew that she was going to be able to handle my pipe. I licked my lips with anticipation. She regained that step she took and got in my face.

"Where are the keys?" She asked.

I got my keys out of my pockets and placed them in her hand. "Don't touch shit in my car." I told her and walked off. I got the shit from JJ and jumped in my car, with Sierra in my passenger seat. We fucked the rest of the weekend and throughout the week. She told me her name and I gave that shit to Tristan and Dexter. They told me about her father and the rest of the family. I told them to make sure that she wasn't sent out here for the Davis crew. They both told me that she was good. I continued fucking her and other random bitches.

Sierra told her father about me and he wanted me to do work for him. I told her that I didn't work for anyone but my family. It was clear that he wanted me to be with his daughter. I just didn't see her that way. She already knew the game and had the knowledge of everything that I needed her to know. But, she didn't make me feel like Joel did. She didn't give me the opportunity to do better. She was content with me like this. I opened the text and read it.

Sierra: Am I coming by tonight

I told her to be waiting for me, with her mouth wide open before I left. I knew her ass was at the club with her friends. Sierra thought that she was the different that I was looking for. Little did she know; her ass was about to get canceled. I ignored her text and placed my

NEICY P.

phone back into my pocket. I walked into the elevator and pressed my floor number. I dropped my head back on the elevator wall. *Straight up bullshit, man.* If it wasn't one thing, it was always another. I had to figure this shit out with Joel quick. That shit she was speaking at the warehouse got me fucked up.

I was going to see my children, whether she liked it or not. I didn't care who her brothers were or if she was crazier than me. Ma fucked up not telling me as well. It was true that I wasn't ready for kids, but they were here, and I hadn't seen them yet. Not even a fucking picture. Come to think of it, I was happy that they stopped her the day she left. I would have slit my own wrist, if she had miscarried my children.

I stood straight up and walked out of the elevator when it got to my floor. No one stayed next to me, so I was the only one on this floor. JJ and Tank came by to use it when they had company. It wasn't too often though. I opened my door and went straight to my bedroom. I fell on my bed and closed my eyes.

Faces. All I saw were faces. I had killed twelve men last week and started this week off with nine. I knew that my body count was going to go up after the shit that happened in the warehouse. The family members of the Stand were going to come for us. And my brothers were right. No one was going to tell us shit. They were going to try a sneak attack on us very soon. I had to regroup and keep my head in the game.

JORDAN

"So, you didn't think that I needed to know that you were taking trips and shit with my son, to the Elites house. Lily, what the fuck is wrong with you?" I shouted.

She had clearly lost her damn mind. It was one thing that she was around them, but to have my son around them was something totally different. I was still trying to get over the fact that Joel was Gage. She could have dealt with me a long time ago. And if she didn't want to deal with me, she could have easily sent her brothers after me. Lily and Ma knew this shit and held it in for what. I understood what Jason was talking about, when he asked Ma about where her loyalty lies. Out of all the women, she should have been the one to tell us when she first found out.

Lily turned and dumped clean clothes on the bed before responded in a harsh whisper.

"Don't be up in here with all that yelling Jo. Turn your volume down, nigga." She replied with too much attitude. "Because at the end of the day, I get to take JoJo wherever the hell I feel like it. He is my son as well. While you spitting and shit all over my comforter, you need to find a way to keep Joel off your ass now that you know who she is." She said and rolled her eyes. Her ass had been bossing up a lot lately. I thought it was the influence that Ma and Tee Glen had on her. The whole time, it was Joel that had been putting all that *I am woman, hear me roar,* shit in her head.

"The hell are you talking about." I yelled again. She looked over at me with a frown on her face. JoJo had fallen asleep in our bed. He was excited that we found out about his cousins. He was ready to invite them over to the house.

"You know that when you threaten an assassin, you are bound to get killed or your ass beat. Joel know how much I love you and that the kids need their father, so she decided that she was going to beat your ass. They all said that you knew the rules." Lily said while folding clothes.

I knew the rules. I didn't need for her smart ass to recite that shit to me. But, how was I supposed to know that Joel was an Elite. I didn't have a comeback for that shit. I was going to deal with that when the time came. She still didn't tell me why she thought it was cool to take our son there. I sat on the edge of the bed and looked up at her. "Are you going to answer my question, Lily?"

"What was the problem with me taking our son to see his cousins? They are fucking family, Jordan. They make each other feel safe. Joel and her brothers treat us like family. Even after the fucked-up shit you did, and the way Jason fucked over Joel, they still accepted us. They hired other guards to protect us when you weren't around. That was the reason why we got away from the hittas that tried to get us the other day. They had our backs. You should be thanking them." Lily replied. My guards did tell me that there were other men shooting at the muthafuckers that tried to kill my family. I was grateful for that, no lie. But, the shit was still fucked up.

"Look, Jordan. I know that this was a secret that I shouldn't have kept. If I thought that Joel was on some scheming shit, I would have told you. But she wasn't. El was here to love and care for your brother. And you took that away from them because you were selfish. You go around saying that it was for the Davis crew. But then again, when you look at it now, who suffered the most from your gain. Your family." Lily told me and trust I heard all of this before. The vision that I saw for the family came with a price that I didn't count on paying.

Lily sat on my lap, rubbing her belly. She grabbed my face, to make sure that I was paying close attention to her next statement. "So, now that you know. What are you going to do about it?" She whispered.

I let out a sigh and placed my hand on her stomach. Pride was a muthafucker. I was man enough to admit that I was the reason why my brother didn't have this moment with Joel. I was also man enough to admit that everything that happened in the past six years was my fault. I knew that we were going to be dealing with a lot of shit after the warehouse incident. But, before we took care of anything, I had to get my brother's family back together. That was my first and only priority.

Sierra

I KNOW his ass didn't ignore my text. Then he had the audacity to turn his phone off. I was on my way from a party that one of my girls was having at JJ's club. He asked me to wait for him after his meeting. I was never the one to sit and wait on a man. I had things to do just like the next one. Oh, if y'all didn't know, I'm Sierra Williams by the way. I was the Princess of my father's empire on the west coast. I had three brothers and two of them already had the north in their hands. My father figured if we could merge with the Davis crew, the world would be ours.

My family was into the gun and the gambling business. We were trying to expand and do more with the drug game but couldn't get reliable resources. My father, Leon Williams sent my brothers, Alan and Brandon to the north to develop some allies and territory. My other brother was somewhere doing him. It didn't matter because we had everything set up and ready. I just had to get Jason on board so that we can get everything started.

I had my eyes on Jason for a while. He was the one that the whole west coast was talking about. Him and that other savage ass nigga called Gage. No one really knew what he looked like. And how my brothers talked about him, I didn't want to meet him. I was fine with my Jason. He didn't believe in titles, but he was mine. He was going to propose, and we were going to move back to my home. I didn't have anything against the east coast, but I was ready to move back to Cali.

I pulled up to Jason's building and parked in my spot next to Jason. I pulled out my phone to call him again and he sent me to voicemail. I got out and walked to the elevator. He was in one of his moods again and I was fine with that. I smiled thinking about how hard he was going to fuck me. The elevator reached the floor. I got off and went to his door. I pulled out my key and unlocked the door. He didn't know that I had made a copy of his key. He always told me to get it from that old bitch at the desk. When I was ready to leave, I had to turn it back in. Like I told y'all, I didn't need permission to see him. He was my man.

I walked and dropped my purse and keys on the table. I went into his bedroom and saw that he was laying on the bed with his hand behind his head, looking at the ceiling. "So, you didn't see me calling your phone." I asked him with my hands on my hips. He didn't bother looking my way, before he responded.

"Don't come in my shit, questioning me about nothing. And how did you get in here anyway?"

"I got the key from the woman downstairs." I told him. He looked over at me this time. I didn't know if he knew the truth or not. He smirked at me and shook his head. Yeah, he knew. He turned his attention back to the ceiling. I walked closer to the bed and looked down on him. I reached for him and he looked back at me with a deadly look.

"I don't want to be bothered right now, go back to the party." He said.

I ignored him and started taking off my clothes. He gave me that don't fuck with me look, but I didn't care. He was gon' give me, me. I didn't play behind his piece. His shit had me speaking Arabic. I stroked his leg and his frown got deeper. I licked my lips and grabbed his stick through his pants.

"How was your meeting?" I asked. He stared at me, ignoring my question. I leaned over him and bit his stick gently while staring at his blazing eyes. "You didn't hear me, huh. I guess I gotta talk into the mic." I told him and pulled it out with no problem. I didn't bother with teasing him because I knew he was already mad at whatever. I swallowed that dreamsicle like I was on the porch to my summer home in California. He closed his eyes and bit down on his bottom lip. Yes sir. His hand grabbed my head and pushed himself deeper into my mouth. I moaned as I felt him hitting my tonsils like it was a punching bag. He grabbed my hair and pulled my head off him. He took my ponytail and wrapped it around his fist.

"This how I asked yo simple ass to wait for me. Open your mouth wide, and don't fucking move." He growled. He got up on his knees and pulled his shorts off. I hoped he didn't think that this was punishment. I opened my mouth with my eyes on his. He licked his lip before pulling it in his teeth. "Don't gag on my shit, either." He told me and slid that shit down my throat. He went in and out at his pace. My tongue slid on the underside of his stick. I closed my mouth tighter. He was getting close, and I was ready for it to melt in my mouth. He didn't give me the chance to. He pulled out of my mouth and let my head go. "Assume the position." He demanded.

I turned around and tooted my ass in the air. I didn't know which hole he was going in. It didn't matter because we had no limits. It was however he wanted it when he was in this mood. I had to make it up to him. I felt something cool hitting my tighter hole. I leaned forward and relaxed every muscle in my body. I took a deep breath in and waited for him to press his thick head inside of me. When the rim of it was in, I let out the deep breath. When I was nice and ready, he picked up the speed and grabbed the headboard so that it could stop hitting the wall. I put my hand between my legs and rubbed on my pearl.

"Oh yes, Jason! Fuck me harder, baby!" I groaned.

He grabbed my waist and did what I asked him to. It sounded like we were fighting in there. I felt the tingling in my legs and knew that I was about to bust all over these sheets. I felt Jason's dick get bigger and knew he was about to bless me with his juice. He never bust inside of me, no matter which hole he was in. I released right before he pulled out and shot that shit on my back. He got out of the bed and went to get some wipes. When he did it in the beginning, I always thought that he was being a good sex partner. I told him how thoughtful he was after we had sex once before. He told me in his Jason way, that it didn't have anything to do with me. He didn't trust no one, after some chick he fucked years back.

He didn't tell me. Everyone knew that it was her that had something to do with his father's death. I didn't have time to argue about me not being her. I was going to show him better. He wiped me off and went to flush it down the toilet. I pulled the covers over my body and waited for him to come back. He got into the bed and pushed me over.

"Next time do what I tell you to do." He told me. I smirked at him and tried to kiss him. "Don't play with me, Sierra. Lay yo ass down and go to sleep." He told me. I wanted those lips on me for a long time. He never went down on me and I thought that he needed time. I kissed him on his shoulder, rolled over and went to sleep.

I woke up to a phone vibrating. I hoped that it wasn't none of my girls that needed a ride home. I wasn't worried about it being another nigga. I didn't fuck around like that. I pulled out my phone and saw that it was four in the morning. I placed my phone back on the nightstand and heard a phone vibrating again. I looked over at the nightstand that was on Jason's side of the bed and saw the lights blinking. I eased out of the bed and walked over to his side. It bet not be no bitches texting him this time of the hour. I snatched his phone and went into the bathroom with it. He never locked his phone and at the time it was a plus for me. I opened his text messages and saw that Jordan was texting him.

Jo: We need to talk. I had invited the kids and Joel over. You need to be here when they come.

I know you lying. What fucking kids? Oh hell no. I erased his messages and all the other messages pertaining to some kids. That was some straight up bullshit. I didn't work this hard to lose my man behind some fucking kids. FUCK THAT! I lifted the toilet seat and dropped that bitch in there. If I could have flushed it down there, I would have. I took it out of the toilet and dried it off with one of the towels. I washed my hand and grabbed his phone. I opened the door and saw him scrolling through another phone.

"Why are you touching my shit?" He whispered. I took my time walking to the bed, thinking of what to say. I didn't come up with nothing but, "When were you going to tell me that you had children?"

"I wasn't planning on telling you shit. Because my business is that. My fucking business. Get yo shit, leave the key, and get the fuck up outta here." He told me with his attention still on his phone. I dropped his phone on the floor and took a step forward. He looked over at me and shook his head. "Don't get fucked up, Sierra." He said.

I was thinking about testing him but the look in his eyes told me to live and fight another day. I picked my clothes up off the floor and start putting them on. I grabbed my phone off the nightstand and walked towards the front door. I took his key off my key ring and dropped it on the table. I was going to give him a week to cool down. I needed to call my father to see if we could come up with a plan about these kids.

JOEL

We were in one of the houses that Poppa purchased for us. We had a home in each state. It wasn't a big mansion like the one we had in Jamaica. It was a six bedroom with five bathrooms, kitchen, game room, pool and two offices. I know y'all think that what I described was a mansion but when you have a family like ours that shit was small.

I was sitting in the family room around my brothers and Poppa. We had to talk about what happened and what to expect next. Poppa didn't give a shit about the repercussions of the murders we committed. He wanted to know what my next step was going to be with his grandbabies.

"So, you wanted that punk ass nigga to live for what." Kymani told me. I didn't want to argue with them about the decision I made. I understood why Kymani and the rest of my family feel the way they felt. My children were their children. They saw Jason as an outsider. We didn't trust people easily. Poppa was friends with Senior for a long time. But all that friendship shit went out the door when he found out what happened between me and Jason. Poppa and Kymel were staring at me. I shook my head and walked over to the window.

"I don't have to answer that, Kymani. I said what I said, and that is all to it." I said with my back turned to them.

"Not on this it ain't. You don't get to make the decision on this by yourself, Joel. We all have raised them babies like they were ours. We have the right to know who you would have in their lives." Kymel spoke. I turned around quickly to face him.

"An yuh decision is to mek dem fatherless." I yelled with my eyes blazing. "Dem ave live dem lives wid theur fada through di stories me an Joyce tell dem. Dem sit an wait fi him fi get well enough to si dem. An yuh wa fi deny dem of dat. Di ongle dream dat dem ave been having since di day dem ask fi him." I smirked at them all before continuing. "Mi wi cut yuh hearts out to mend fi dem." Kymel stood up knowing that he had a better chance standing than sitting. I knew it looked like I was ready to tear their asses open, but I had complete control over myself. I was angry, yeah. But not ready to kill someone, yet. I took in a deep breath and maintained eye contact with Kymel. "I understand that you all are worried. But, what you must understand is, as their mother, I would never put them in harm's way. When we do this, if the children look or feel uncomfortable, we will leave. And I will take care of Jason. I don't need help with that." I said.

Poppa looked at me with a frown on his face. "Eff dem hurt mi babies El, yuh wi suffa." He told me. I nodded my head knowing that I would die a slow death for them. I turned and walked back to the window. Kymani sat down next to Poppa, while Kymel walked over to me. "What about the other Davis boy? The one that started all this shit. Do you want him to live too?" He asked.

Kymel and I was always close. When he came to visit me, he always stayed longer than Kymani. We hung out and did a lot of stuff that I wanted to do. Kymani told me that I was messing up his style. He couldn't date or bring his girls around me. I would scare them off by flicking my knife or start talking about how much good it would feel to bathe in their blood. He would try to put on a front like he cared and didn't know what got into me. When they left, he fell out laughing and went out to pick up a different girl. He wouldn't bring her back to our house. My mother didn't mind them being there. She just didn't

NEICY P.

want them with all of that activity in her house. She loved them like they were her own. Once she passed away, Kymel stayed in the house with me until I graduated from high school. Kymani was back and forth to the states. He was trying to build a name for himself. When he was done accomplishing one of his goals, he came back home and gave Kymel a break from my drama.

I looked over at him and reached out to grab his hair. "That is a dance that I plan on taking as soon as everything is settled. He won't get away with threatening me." I said. Kymel wanted to disagree with me. But, I already called dibbs on that kill a long time ago. I knew if I killed Jordan, I was going to have to take the whole Davis crew out. So, I decided to beat the shit out of him.

My phone began to ring, and I saw that it was Joyce. I'm pretty sure that they went home and told her about who I am. She also had to reveal what she knew and that probably set Jason off. I hoped he didn't put his hands on her. "Hey, Ma-Ma. Is everything ok?" I answered.

"Yes, sweetheart. Everything is fine." She let out a sigh. "I told him about my relationship with the children. He didn't take it well." She said sadly.

"We knew that he wouldn't Ma-Ma." I replied. "Are you ok? Did he hurt you?" I asked.

"Not physically. He did ask me where my loyalty lies and that fuck me up. I don't ever want my children to think that I don't have their back." Joyce told me.

"Don't do it, Ma-Ma. Don't let that fool or anyone else make you feel guilty about being there for your grandchildren." I told her getting angry.

"I know Joel. We just have to come up with a way for him to see them. Maybe they could give him that peace that they give you." Joyce replied.

I dropped my head back and thought of what she was saying. I wanted Jason to have a relationship with our children but the way that he was acting was making it hard for that to happen. Ma-Ma always tried to get me to talk to Jason. Whenever I did, he was fucking with that hoe, Sierra. I ain't gon' lie and say that I wasn't mad about him fucking her. I was pissed. He laid up with Sierra without a care in the world. I had to sit my feelings aside and think about what was best for my children. I looked back at my brothers and father. Knowing that after the decision was made, we couldn't turn back or change nothing. Poppa nodded his head, telling me to continue.

"When do you want us to come over, Ma-Ma?" I asked her.

"Thank you, baby." She said with relief. "I will talk to his brothers, so that we can come up with a way to get him over here. I will call you later with the plans." Ma-Ma said and hung up the phone.

I placed my phone back into my pocket. "Your brothers are going with you." Poppa said without room to argue. I wasn't planning on it. I knew that my Poppa had to return to Jamaica for some business. He knew that my brothers could handle whatever. I smiled over at Kymel and turned to walk out of the room. My babies were going to be happy to hear the news. Ever since Mason got the video of his father, he had been watching it over and over. He was obsessed with it. He had seen pictures of Jason before, but the live feed and hearing his voice was something different.

When Madison first saw a picture of Jason, she knew that she could keep him off the ledge. She would rub her face on the picture that she kept on the side of her bed and whisper to him that everything was going to be alright. They loved him more than anything in the world and I was proud of that. I was proud of a lot of things pertaining to my children. Kymel and Kymani had been training them since they were able to talk. I taught them how to read, speak, and write in four different languages. Because they weren't strong yet, my brothers made them study the anatomy of the human body. They learned the vulnerable points on the body that with a little pressure, would bring anyone to their knees. We all knew that their mentality was like mine and my brothers. Adding Jason fuckedupness with that, only made their shit a lot worse.

They both showed signs of it when a woman that Kymel was dating, accidentally stepped on Madison's hand while we were at a picnic. Mason stared up at her with the look his father had given many. The woman squatted down to check Madison's hand. Madison yanked her hand from her and wiped the tears from her eyes. She apologized and reached out to her. Mason grabbed her hand and stabbed her in the wrist with a fork. We weren't shocked at the behavior, because it was something that we all would have done at that age. We were some messed up kids, y'all.

Kymani bit a piece of his nanny's face off because she didn't want to give him juice when he was three. Kymel locked their other nanny outside the yard, where Poppa kept them mean ass dogs. She got bit up and was mauled to death. Poppa stopped hiring people to babysit them. When I came along, my brothers became overprotective and didn't want anyone around me. I was like that with them and Poppa.

When I was four, I poisoned Poppa's girlfriend, Tricia. She also had stab wounds in her face. She was annoying and was only with him for the money. There were other reasons that brought that on. More was for my mother. She had been waiting on Poppa to come to her and he never did. He always had these different women in his house, trying to be my friend. Poppa found her body in the pantry with me. I was sitting on the side of her body eating cookies. He started my training with my Parrain. It was hard, but I liked it.

I got to their room and knocked on their door.

"Come in." Madison's sweet voice came through the door. I opened it and saw them both sitting on the bed watching television.

"Hey guys, we need to talk." I told them. Mason jumped off the bed and turned off the television.

"Is everything ok, Mommy?" Mason asked with concern.

I smiled down at him and grabbed his hand. We walked to the bed and sat next to Madison, who gave me her undivided attention.

"Everything is fine, my Lovies. I just want to talk to you guys about your father." I said.

Mason's eyes lit up with joy. His shoulder-length, blonde dreads were hanging neatly around his around face. His hazel eyes sparkled like mine. Madison's hair was natural and was placed in two large puffs. Her hair was blonde as well. She looked like a sweet angel.

"Are we going today?" Madison asked in her soft voice.

"No, but I am thinking that it will be later this week. Ma-Ma is setting things up. You will get to meet your uncles and you will get to see your cousin, JoJo." I told them.

"Yes! I miss my cousin." Mason said jumping up and down.

When Lily came over with JoJo, he would run straight to Mason's room. They would be up there playing and talking. Madison could go in there, but she always came down with the women. She told us that Mason needed his boy time with JoJo.

"I am pretty sure that he misses the both of you as well. But, our main goal is to see your father. Now, we talked about Daddy's mood and what might happen when he sees y'all. And if there is a moment when you guys feel uncomfortable and want to leave, let me know, ok. We can always try another time." I told them both.

I didn't like sugarcoating things with my kids. They knew everything about me and their uncles. They knew about Jason as well. We didn't worry about them telling anyone because they knew what would happen if they do.

"I'm not gonna want to leave. I want to help Daddy get better, so that he can come move in with us and watch me and Mason hit our targets. I think that he would be proud of us. Don't you think, Mommy?" Madison said.

"Yes, Lovies. Daddy would be so proud of you." I told them.

Mason grabbed his phone and showed me his wallpaper on his phone. It was a picture of Jason in the warehouse. He unlocked it and it was a picture of the three of us in Jamaica. "Mommy, when we get there, can we take a picture of all of us. I would like to have one for my wallpaper." He asked.

I nodded my head and pulled him to me. Madison wrapped her arms around me as well. I kissed them both on their heads and pulled back. "Now that that is settled, did you guys finish your lessons today?" I asked them. They had to write a story in Japanese and finish some math problems on their tablets. Everything was timed. They did well, always.

"Yes, ma'am. We did it this morning, so that we can have more time with Uncle Mani. We are playing with knives this evening. That's what Madison love. I like the hand to hand combat the most. I get to take cheap shots at Uncle Mel. I pretend like I don't know what I am doing, so that we can do it again." He said with a huge smile on his face. "Are you coming to watch?" Mason said.

"Of course, baby." I replied.

Madison jumped off the bed and went to her closet to change for their session. I usually didn't attend their training sessions with my brothers. Once before, I watched them and almost took Mani out when he hit him. Mason jumped up and started attacking Mani with me. Mel stood on the sideline laughing with Madison. They knew that we weren't planning on hurting him. I was warning him to be more careful. Madison opened a hidden door in her closet. She pulled out a familiar black case and brought it to the bed. She lifted the lid open and pulled out six small knives. These were the knives that Poppa gave me when I was young.

"Come on, Mommy. Uncle Mel hates when we are late. He makes us run." Madison told me. "I hate running because it always makes me sweaty."

Mason laughed at her. "Yeah Mommy, you should see her. She starts whining and talks about how her hair is going to frizz up. Uncle Mel always falls for it, but she threatens to tell on Uncle Mani. Poppa came out there once and cursed him out."

"You can't do that Madison. You can't be all cute in battle." I told her.

"Yes, I can. You did it in the video at the warehouse. You looked beautiful." She said and walked out the door.

"Yeah, Mommy. You looked great. Daddy couldn't take his eyes off you." Mason said, following behind his sister.

If they only knew that he was looking at me for a different reason. I got off the bed and went downstairs. Kymel was standing with the children telling them how his time was important. Madison told him that they were late because I was talking to them about their father. He looked up at me and I smirked.

"Alright, I still need my ten laps around the yard. Then I want you two to stretch and do practice throws." He told them. Mason grabbed his sister's hand and walked her to the back door.

"You are not bringing your ass out there with us." Kymel told me. I shook my head.

"Why I can't go?" I asked already knowing why.

"We are training with knives, El. I don't need you warning me about shit by throwing one of your favorite blades at me. Plus, they train better when you are not around. If I tell Madison to do something and she don't want to do it, she will look over at you and give you them puppy dog eyes. I already gotta watch my back with Mason." He told me.

Before I could respond, my phone started ringing. I pulled it out and watched Kymel use that distraction to start his training with the children. I looked at the screen and saw that it was Jordan. I really wasn't for his shits and giggles. I took a deep breath and answered it.

"Yes Jordan."

"Hi, Joel. Do you have a minute to talk?" He asked.

"Yeah, I have a minute. What's up?" I replied.

"I wanted to know if you could bring my niece and nephew over to meet their family." Jordan answered.

"Does Jason know that you are calling me?" I asked instead.

"No, he doesn't." He said letting out a deep breath. "Look Joel, I know that you may hate me for what I had done to Jason. I am trying to right my wrongs and bring his family together. He needs to see his children. And whether he wants to believe it or not, he needs to see you as well. Not Gage, but the Joel that he had met in the grocery store. I am ready to do whatever you need me to do to make this happen Joel." He practically begged.

I walked to the back door and watched my children train with my brother. Madison was throwing the knife at the tree and hitting the target. Mason was swinging his at a mannequin that had the outline of all the major arteries. Any parent would see this and say that I was wrong for raising them this way. In the business that we were in, we had to prepare them for the worse. If Poppa didn't train me so early, those men would have raped my momma and done Gods know what to me. I needed to know that they were safe when I wasn't around. Mani and Mel had their businesses along with Poppa. They didn't mind my children's company. It gave them a reason to be kids again. Poppa was sitting around playing video games with Mason. Mel and Mani did tea parties with Madison. We all went on picnics and vacationed together. Madison and Mason were all our soft spots. They were able to bring us out of our dark moods with a smile on their face. The feeling that I got was indescribable.

It was a feeling that I wanted to share with their father. "When."

"Tomorrow at one. We will be at my parents' home," Jordan answered.

"Ok, but Jordan." I said and let some of that darkness come through. "If anything goes wrong while we there, the beating that I owe you will be worse than what I had planned." I told him and hung up the phone. I watched them train until it was time for them to come in. Madison walked in and went straight upstairs. She was going to take a bath. Mason looked drained and tired. "Hey little man. How did it go?" I asked him.

"I'm ok, Mommy. Don't baby me?" He said and moved out of the way when I tried to grab his hair. He was always my big boy. "Well, I got some good news for you. We are going to see your daddy tomorrow." I said. His face brightened up and he leaped into my arms. He pulled back and kissed me on the nose. "You are the best Mommy ever." He told me. Right then and there, I knew that I made the right decision.

JASON

"Ahhhhh!" Maurice's punk ass yelled.

Maurice and two other men were caught stealing from our main warehouse downtown. I didn't know if they thought that we were too busy to notice, but I caught onto that shit the first time they did it. I was just trying to see how long they were going to do it. They didn't notice that I went and changed up the product that they had stolen. A bunch of dumbasses that I was happy to get rid of. All three men were hanging upside down with their shirts off. I was making small cuts all over their bodies.

"Why do you think stealing from us is acceptable, Mo?" I asked him as I sliced into his fat ass skin. The other two men were barely breathing. So, I took my time with Maurice. I needed him to last longer than the others. With all the shit that I was going through, his ass was about to suffer. I went around his back and made a nice incision on his spine. He screamed out again. "Answer me, ya big bitch. Why steal from us?"

"I'm sorry man. It won't happen again." He cried out.

"Yeah it won't happen again because- "I tried to reply but was cut off by my phone. I pulled it out and saw that it was Jordan. I ignored him and placed my phone back into my pocket. "Like I was saying," I began to say and felt my phone vibrating. I took it out and opened the text message that he left.

Jo: We need to talk, bruh. It is important.

I tossed my phone on the table where all my gadgets were. I hated being interrupted while torturing muthafuckers. "So, you were saying how sorry you were. I don't think you understand the meaning of that word. Because if you were so sorry, you wouldn't have done it the second and third time. Now, I can see that these little cuts that I'm making on your thick ass body ain't doing shit." I told him and reached for my hunter's blade.

It was thicker and sharper than the one I was using before. I surveyed it and thought of the many ways that I was going to cut his ass up. I walked over to his body with a deadly smirk on my face. I had been needing to make a kill since I found out about Joel. Sierra was another fucking case that I had to deal with on another date. Sierra's ass was hardheaded. She was going to show up again after I told her not to. She thought because of the clout that her father and brothers had around the states, it was going to make me think twice about treating her the way I did.

Nope.

Fuck her and her family. They didn't want my troubles. I took the blade and peeled his skin off from the bottom of his stomach to the top of his chest, like I was peeling a potato. His skin fell off. I continued that for more than an hour, while my phone continued vibrating. I walked over to it and threw it to the wall. I saw the text messages that Sierra erased. I didn't know how to feel about that. I was a father to two children that knew everything about me. What were their thoughts about me? It couldn't be far off, if Joel told them who she was. But they were around her their whole lives. They got used to what she was. It was different with me.

They heard about me but didn't know me. I wasn't there when she felt their first kick or any other movements. I wasn't there when they entered the world. I didn't hear the first word they spoke or the first step they made. Birthdays. Christmases. Father's Day or any other holiday I missed because of her selfishness. Yeah, we had to talk and if it was some shit I didn't want to hear, we are going to do more than talking. I was so far over the edge, that it would be hard for anyone to bring me down.

I heard the chains of the locks drop from one of the men's arm. My ass was daydreaming so hard, that I didn't know that he got loose. I came back to the present and felt the blood running down my arm. I had the whole blade in Maurice's stomach. I had stabbed him at least twelve times. You can hear him choking off his own blood. I snatched it out of his body and threw it to the other man's back. He reached the door, right when it opened. Jordan and Joseph were walking in with their eyes on me.

"I know you saw me calling you, bruh." Jordan yelled out. Joseph pulled out his gun and unloaded a full clip in the man's face. "Come on, man. Leave they asses here for the cleanup crew. We gotta go. Joel is on her way to the house with your children. Go clean yourself up. We can ride over there together." Joseph said while stepping over the body.

I pulled my gun out and shot the other two men in the head. I needed fresh bodies now, to relieve the stress. I looked over at my brothers and their asses stopped walking. "Y'all know how I hate being interrupted. Which of you gon' volunteer to make me feel better." I told them.

Jordan passed his gun to Joseph. He put his hand up and started walking forward. "I know that I am the last person that you want to see, J. But it is time to put all our differences aside and prepare you for your children."

"Prepare me. Nigga, let's be real. You can't prepare me for shit, Jo. You are the last person I would accept advice from. You think shit changed because I saved you at that meeting. Nah, mi boy. Everything is still the same over here." I said while jumping off the stage.

Jordan let out a sigh and took off his shirt. I saw some new tattoos on his body. Pops' name was on the inside of his right arm and Ma's name was on his left. Joseph's name was around his left wrist and my name was around his right. The nigga looked like he got buff a little, but that shit wasn't hitting on nothing if his technique was the same. I got in front of him and his phone started ringing. He passed it to JJ without looking at it. JJ looked at it and passed it back to him.

JoJo's picture was flashing on his screen. Jo swiped it and answered, "What's up, Lil Man?"

"Hey Daddy. Are you with Uncle Jason?" His little voice came through the phone.

Jo looked over at me and answered hesitantly. "Yeah JoJo, why?"

"I just wanted to tell him some of Mason's and Madison's favorite things, so that he can go and get them before they come over. Can I talk to him please?" He said in a rushed tone. Jo looked over at me waiting for me to react to what his son said.

Mason and Madison. I got a girl and boy. Wow. I knew my weapons collection had to be on point now. Because if my baby girl looked anything like her mother, those lil niggas was going to be after her. I was going to have to call Marquel quick. He was my weapons supplier. Anything that I needed, his ass got it for me and for a great price. Shit. A fucking daughter. We weren't used to having small girls around. That mean that we had to watch how we talked around each other.

I held out my hand for the phone. When Jo placed it in my hand, I grabbed his wrist and gut-punched his ass and snatched the phone from his hand right before he fell to his knees.

"Muthafucker," he wheezed out.

"Take that shit like a man. He barely hit yo ass." JJ said while examining the gun Jo put in his hand.

"Fuck you, and you ain't taking my shit." He said while sitting in one of the theater chairs. I put the phone to my ear and talked to my nephew. "What type of stuff do they like, JoJo?

"Hey Uncle Jason. Do you have a pen and paper?" He answered.

"Nah, but I'll remember it." I replied.

"Ok, Mason likes all types of video games. His favorite is Gears of War. He plays that with our uncles and sometimes with Grandpa as well. He like cookies and cream ice cream and chocolate chip cookies. Oh yeah, he asked Aunt Joel for a Ruger LCRx .38 Special. Uncle Mani let him train with his, but he wanted his own. Madison loves her dolls.

They had to be black dolls because that is all she plays with. She like strawberry shortcake ice cream and she loves to draw. Madison also wanted a WASP injector knife. They want some other things, but you can ask them more about it when they get here." He finished.

I looked over at my brothers. They both had their mouths opened with surprise. My children wanted weapons. That was something else I needed to add to the list to be pissed off about. If my kids were training, I wanted to be the one to do it. I took a deep breath in and let it out slowly. I didn't want my nephew to hear how I was feeling. He was just trying to help. "Good looking out lil man." I told him.

"I wasn't doing it for you, Uncle Jason. I wanted Mason and Madison to have those things. I thought that they deserved it and since Aunt Joel wasn't getting them. I was hoping that you would so that they wouldn't mind staying. Can you make sure to get them?" He answered truthfully.

I smiled and was happy that he had a relationship with them. When we were kids, Jordan and Joseph always talked about raising their kids together. We were trying to keep the family safe. I didn't talk too much about it because I didn't want any children. I never thought I would find someone to have my children with. Until Joel. I cleared my throat and continued talking to JoJo. "Thank you, anyway, JoJo." I told him and hung up the phone. I walked back towards the table with my mind set on what I was going to do next.

"Come on, Jason. You gotta be there for them. Ma told me that they were waiting their whole life for you to get well enough to meet you. Don't ignore them man. You'll regret it in the end." He said still sitting. I shook my head and picked up some things from the table.

"I know Jordan. I'll be there. I gotta put the order in for my children." I told him.

"Thank you, Jesus. I thought we were going to have to drag your ass out here." JJ replied with relief.

"You and who else were going to drag me out here." I asked. I won't lie to y'all and tell you that my brothers were weak men. They had been my sparring partners for years. Jordan and Jason looked like they were getting bigger than I was. I didn't care. The way that I had been feeling for the past five, almost six years, they were going to need a tank to remove me out of here.

"Oh, we brought reinforcements." Jo said.

The door opened and in comes Ma, Tee Glen, and my cousins. Tee Glen and Ma were the only ones bold enough to jump in my shit when I wasn't right. Tee Glen stood at the door and yelled out to me.

"Let's go boy, we don't have all day. Them children are coming over in the next two hours. Me and your mother wanted to have something cooked before they come over." She said and turned around with her cigarette in her hand. She blew the smoke out and waited for me to meet her at the door. I looked over to my mother and told her in so many words that I didn't know what was supposed to happen next. She walked over to me and smiled.

"Your father always thought you were stronger than the average man. All the worries that you have, let that shit go. Trust me when I tell you that they have been waiting for you to come to your senses." Ma told me. She grabbed my hand and that move felt foreign. The only hand that I used to hold like this was Joel's. Ma squeezed it gently and tugged at it. Like a little boy, I followed Ma and the rest of the family out of the door. Everyone was parked around my car. Jo got in the driver's seat in my car while JJ got into the back behind the passenger seat. They were making sure that I got to the house.

"See you later," Ma told me. She grabbed my face and stared into my eyes. I tried to look back into hers, but it was hard. I knew that I disappointed her in many ways. I wished that I was the man that she raised me to be. She shook her head as if she heard my thoughts. "And I love you still." She whispered and kissed me on the forehead.

I nodded my head and jumped in the car. I went into my bag and pulled out another phone. I programmed it and called Marquel. I didn't want to show up to the house empty-handed. Marquel answered on the second ring, "Yo."

"Are you in my city?" I asked him.

"I am by the Harbor. Come thru." He responded.

"Bet." I said and hung up the phone. "Go to the Harbor right quick. I need to pick up some things." I told Jo.

Jo made the left and headed in the direction of Harbor. I hoped that fool knew that we still weren't cool. I think I am going to need to see his ass bleed before I trust him again. I had always blamed myself for Pops' death. The look on my family's faces would always be a memory that I couldn't get rid of. I didn't want to cause my mother any more pain by taking out her son. That was why I stayed my distance and limited our conversation. If I was with him too long, I'd get the urge to wrap my hands around his neck. JoJo was another reason for Jo being alive and well. I didn't want my nephew to experience the same pain I did. I wasn't taking Pops' death well as a man. I didn't want to inflict that type of sadness on JoJo.

"Good, I need another gun. I been wanted to call Marquel." JJ said in the back. I turned and looked out of the window. I thought of the things that I would say when I saw my children for the first time. When I was thinking of having kids with Joel, I hoped that they were like her. Sweet and understanding. But, her ass was worse than me. My kids couldn't escape the shit if they wanted to. They had some fucked-up uncles and grandparents.

Jo pulled up at the Harbor and cut off the engine. He turned towards me and started talking. "J, I just wanted to say,"

"Nah nigga. Are you stupid? We are meeting up with our weapons expert and you decide now to confess some shit to him. You better wait until he is in his happy place." JJ said and jumped out of the car. I looked over at Jo to see if he wanted to finish the conversation. He shook his head and got out of the car, with me doing the same. The warehouse door opened, and Malik was standing there. He was Marquel's brother. His ass was crazy like me. Marquel was too, but he didn't do the torturing shit.

"Whoa, what's up with you, Malik?" JJ dapped him off.

"Nothing. Chilling out here. What you fools are up to?" He asked. We bumped fists after Jo greeted him.

"We just need some new shit." I said and walked in. Marquel and his other brother that looked like Jon B, was standing next to some tables. He had everything laid out and ready for us.

"You going to war, nigga. You need some help." Marquel asked. He was always down for whatever. His brothers were some loyal ass niggas.

"Nah, I needed to pick something out for my children." I said after dapping them off.

"Children!" The three of them yelled.

"Yeah, I done fucked around and got a set of twins, man." I said awkwardly.

"Damn. Your baby mama gotta be a bad chick to have your children. Is it anybody we know?" Marquel asked.

"I don't think so." JJ said while handling a Marlin BFR.

"What are your babies' name, man?" Malik asked.

"Mason and Madison," I said that shit with pride.

"OHH shit, you talking about Shadow and Reap niece and nephew. You fucked around and got Gage pregnant, nigga." Marquel said with surprise.

"How the fuck you know them?" Jo asked.

"Man, I told y'all I supply all. I go to them every week. The last couple of times I went over there, the children were looking at some of my merchandise. I was impressed with how much shit they knew. If you are here for them, I know exactly what you are looking for." He said and nodded over to Jon B. He went upstairs to retrieve what Marquel was asking for.

"Bruh, you got Gage." Malik said.

"She wasn't Gage when I met her. I just found out who she really was a couple of days ago." I told them.

"Y'all two are meant to be together. Both of y'all are some crazy muthafuckers, with some crazy ass children." Marquel told me.

"I know you ain't talking. Says the nigga that is loving on his sister." JJ said and laughed.

"Fuck you, boy. She ain't my sister." Marquel said getting angry. We all started laughing at him. His story was all over the place. Don Washington was the founder of his gun business. He wanted to leave it to his children but fucked around and had six girls with five different women. He didn't want to leave his business to his girls, so he left it to their brothers instead. Marquel and Malik were the head ones in charge. Jon B was next along with Chavez, Brent, and a lil savage nigga, Keith. Marquel was in love with the youngest daughter Cherrie. The nigga was so gone behind her, he had her name tatted on his back.

"How is business going?" I changed the subject.

"Business is good. I got a couple ventures in the west. My people that stay up north said the Williams boys had been trying to start noise up there. They ain't hitting on shit, though. We already moving in their territory. The shit ain't no secret. A lot of his customers made it known that they were going to make moves my way. William's hoe ass started blackmailing them. Talking about, he gon' send one of his Fed buddies their way. I still supply them on the slick, though." Marquel answered.

"And you said he know already." I asked, intrigued by what I was hearing.

"Yeah that bitch know. I'm gon' make it louder so that he could hear me though." He replied.

"Well I think I can help you with that. I used to fuck with his daughter. I'm pretty sure his ass is going to call me after she tells him how I dismissed her ass. I'll let him know."

"Yeah. Good looking out." He said and dapped me off again.

Jon B came down the stairs with a suitcase in his hand. Marquel's sister, Sakia was following behind him. Sakia was just like the niggas. Whenever you saw Marquel or Malik, you saw her.

"What's up fellas?" She spoke.

"What's up Ki?" Me and Jo responded.

JJ didn't speak. His ass was still salty behind some shit that happened way back. Sakia had pulled a chick that JJ was feeling. His bitter ass still couldn't let that shit go.

Jon B opened the suitcase and turned it around for us to check out what was inside. It was a customized blue Ruger with *Mason's Piece* written on it. As bad as I wanted to, I didn't pick it up. I wanted him to be the first to hold it. I looked next to it and saw the knife that my baby girl wanted. The Wasp injector knife was also customized with a purple and pink handle, with diamonds encrusted in it. She also had writing on it. *Daddy's Baby Girl.* My heart melted instantly. They were just like me.

"Damn, the fuck you got these from." JJ asked. He was about to pick baby girl knife up. I slapped his hand and closed the case.

"Don't touch her shit, nigga." I told him and picked up the case. I pulled out my black card and was ready to swipe it. Marquel shook his head. "No need, bruh. I owed them this for their birthday. Gage told their uncles that she didn't want them with it yet."

"Nah, they are getting these today." I told him and grabbed the suitcase. I was feeling some type of way, not knowing their birthday. I had to get them some more shit. "Thanks, Quel."

"No problem. Anything for my mini killers." He said.

"Hey, I want one of those knives for myself. Customized and all." JJ said.

"Not from me. That is a one of a kind treat. You better pick something else." Malik answered. I walked out the warehouse and back to the car. We all hopped back in and rode to my parents' home. I was still a little nervous about meeting them. I leaned my head back and closed my eyes. I took nice deep breaths in and let them out slowly. My phone went off. I took it out and it was Sierra calling me.

"Hey, you better tell Sierra to stop calling you before Joel fuck both of y'all up. You know we don't do that step-parent shit." JJ said over my back.

"Sit your ass back and mind your business." I told him and cut my phone off. I didn't know what type of relationship I was going to have with Joel. I knew for a fact that she wasn't gon' bring other niggas around my children. Her brothers or father wouldn't approve of that shit. We pulled up at the house and saw two white Escalades parked in the front. I jumped out of the car ready to meet my babies. I walked in the house with the suitcase in my hand. JJ and Jo were right behind me. They were eager to see what they looked like. I went into the room that I heard talking in.

Shadow and Reaper were standing over Joel. We made eye contact and I saw the woman that I fell in love with. Her hair was up in a ponytail. Joel had on a red dress with no straps. She had her pretty feet out in some sandals. No makeup. All natural.

Fuck!

I felt those feelings slipping back in. I took a step towards her and Reaper stepped in front of her. I placed the suitcase on the floor next to Ma. She was sitting on the loveseat next to Tee Glen. Tank and Tristian were standing behind them. I didn't want to start shit up, but I wasn't going to back down from nothing, either. I heard Joel whisper out to him.

"Kymani, don't." She said. Shadow put his hand on her shoulder to calm her. I knew that I had to deal with the consequences of messing around with Joel. It was another code we respected. If you dated the daughter of an assassin, you gotta get yo ass beat by the father or the brothers if she had any. It was a way to see if you were worthy of her.

He stared me down with his dreads pushed back from his face with a bandanna. Tank and Tristan walked around the couch and stood on each side of my brothers. Ma and Tee Glen stood up as well. Those two were my ride and die for real. Tee Glen had her piece in her hand waiting for something to pop off. Joel stood and got in front of her brother. "I told yuh, we not here for that. Calm yourself, Kymani." She told him. He ignored her and tried to push her out of the way. She turned and frowned at him. "Yuh playing wid mi Kymani." She told him. He finally looked down at her and stepped back slowly. I guess he didn't want to deal with Gage. She turned to face me. Damn, she was beautiful. There was no denying that. Shadow moved to get in front of her, but the look she gave him stopped him dead. She shook her head and faced me again. "Hi Jason," she said softly. I didn't bother speaking back. I wasn't for the small talk.

"Where are my children?" I asked her straight out.

She smiled friendly at me before responding. "Our children, Jason. And they are upstairs with JoJo."

"You know we need to talk about this, right." I told her.

"Why? I mean what is it that we have to talk about?" She said confusingly.

"You know muthafuckin well, what we need to talk about. You

were pregnant with my children and didn't decide to call me or tell me when yo ass was here. That's ratchet, bruh. I thought that you were better than that. Clearly, you are just like these other dizzy ass broads." I spoke with so much anger. I knew what my mother and Aunt said about her keeping the children, when she didn't have to. But, when she decided that she was going to keep them, I should have received a phone call.

"Nah, fuck that shit, Joel. He ain't gon' be talking to you like you didn't save his life and the lives of his brothers. He better sho sum goddamn respect or mi gon' knock his fucking head off." Shadow stepped forward and yelled.

"Kymel, mi babies are here," she whispered with her eyes still on mine. "I told yuh that I could handle it. So, let me handle it." She told him. Shadow didn't move. He stood next to his sister, grilling me. "The day I found out that I was pregnant was the day Pops was murdered. You threatened me the same day and lost complete control of yourself. You began killing families and any other person that got in your way. You created enemies around the world. And you standing here wondering why I didn't tell you about them. The reason is simple. You weren't in your right state of mind to accept our children. You were looking for blood, not love. You were looking to murder your grief away, not a reason to live afterwards or to make Pops proud. The assassins that were sent out to kill Jordan's son found out about the twins. They came for our children, based on the shit that you had done over the years. That is far from ratchet, nigga. That is me, looking out for our children. Check yo words before spitting that shit at me. You don't want to get misunderstood." She said to me with fire in her eyes.

Before I could say another word, we heard footsteps coming down the stairs. We all faced the door and waited for a face to appear. JoJo came strolling in. "Daddy guess what, Mason got me an Xbox One."

"You have one of those already, son." Jo answered.

"But, not like this one," JoJo said with a smile.

Another face came into view. A face that looked just like mine and my brothers. His eyes landed straight on me. I can see that he had already surveyed the room before walking in. It was something that had to be taught to him to do. Not many men knew to do shit like that. Already, he was making me proud. Mason was staring at me like he was star struck. He had his blonde dreads braided up into a ponytail. He had on some khaki pants with a red collar shirt. My son.

Before I can say anything to him, another face appeared in the doorway and my heart stopped. Baby girl was a vision for sore eyes. She also had on a red dress, but she had straps and flowers on hers. Her hair was also braided up into a ponytail. She had small gold hoop earrings in her ear. She looked like me and Joel, mixed. Joel took a step back to let me get the full effect of this. Mason grabbed his sister's hand and pushed her forward. Madison walked towards me. I kneeled before her to match her height. Baby girl wasn't nervous at all. You could see the confidence in her walk.

Once she got in front of me, she showed me her hands. I smiled and nodded my head. Madison stepped forward and placed her hands on my face. I stared into her hazel eyes. She smiled with deep dimples.

"Hi Daddy. I'm Madison Jace Davis. Are you feeling well today?" She asked. Hearing her voice and concern for me melted my troublesome heart.

"I am ok, baby girl. Are you ok?" I replied to her.

She inhaled a deep breath and let it go. "I am good, Daddy. I missed you so much." She said with tears in her eyes.

I didn't know how she could miss someone that she had never seen before. She stepped closer to me and wrapped her arms around my neck. I could hear the movement behind my back. I knew that they were worried, but they didn't need to be. I would never put a hand on my baby girl. I gently squeezed her until I felt another hand on my arm. I looked at it, and saw that my son, Mason was standing behind his sister. She pulled back and smiled at her brother.

"It's ok, Mason. Daddy is really good." Madison told him and stepped back.

I stood up and looked at him. He didn't have the innocent expression on his face like Madison. He was checking me out. He wanted to know if I was ok. I stuck my hand out and waited for him to take it.

NEICY P.

When he saw what he needed to, he placed his hand in mine and squeezed it. He maintained eye contact and introduced himself.

"My name is Mason Jason Davis. I am the oldest." He told me.

"It is nice to meet you son," I replied.

I pulled him to me and hugged him tightly. The way he stood before me, made me even prouder. I knew that, that had everything to do with the people across the room. My children were strong and by the way they talked, you could tell that they were well-educated.

"You see, Mommy. I told you that I was the key to bring Daddy back to life." Madison said. I grabbed baby girl too and pulled her into the hug with me and her brother. This was that unconditional love that Pops felt from us.

"You were right, Lovey. You were right." Joel said with a smile.

JOEL

I sat and watched my children talk to Jason for hours. Madison brought a book that carried photos of them since they were small. Jason sat and listened while they explained every photo to him. He didn't give the children a chance to talk to anyone else. They introduced themselves to their uncles and went right back to their father.

When we sat to eat, they sat on both sides of him. Jason was so excited that he didn't touch his food. His phone had been vibrating since he got here. I knew it was that chick, Sierra that he was fooling around with. I had to remind myself that it wasn't about me and him. Either way it goes, he was gon' have to give her up. Madison didn't play being second to no one. All the men in her life put her in their number one slot. You could see how JJ was falling in that category as well.

Kymani and Kymel joined us for dinner. They were making threatening faces at Jo and Jason. I think they wanted Jason more. They didn't like the fact that he could be easily manipulated by his brother. Kymel already told Kymani if they were in that situation, he would had killed him with ease. Kymani told him that he wouldn't have to, because he would have killed himself. Our relationship was tight, don't get me wrong. We just didn't play that using each other for anything.

We were now sitting back in the family room. Jason pulled out the suitcase that he walked in with.

"Hey, I got a surprise for you two." He told the twins.

They stood next to him and waited for Jason to open the case. When he did, the twins smiled down at whatever was in the case.

"Oh, wow Daddy. This is exactly what I wanted." Madison screeched out. She pulled out that fucking knife I told my brothers not to get her. If Jason got her that, I knew that he got Mason that gun. Mason pulled out the Ruger and started surveying it.

"Thanks Dad. Hey, can you take me to the shooting range for target practice. I need to break this in." Mason said. Jason smiled at him and nodded his head.

"Sure son." He said.

I didn't want to argue the fact that they were not supposed to have this until they got a little older. I wanted this to be a moment that the three of them would remember. Kymani's work phone went off and he walked out the door. JJ was trying to show Madison some moves with her knife, while Mason showed his gun off to JoJo.

"Wow, this is so cool. I can't wait 'til I get my own gun." He said, looking over at his parents.

"Don't even try it." Lily responded. She didn't agree with how I was raising the twins and that was fine. She just didn't want Mason to have the wrong influence on him. That was why Mason asked to buy game consoles or the other newest gadgets for JoJo. Mason looked over at me and that was a sign letting me know that we had to buy JoJo another gift, since he couldn't have the gun. I smiled at my son. He had a good heart, along with his sister when it came to their cousin.

Jason walked over to me and stood by my side. "Thank you." He said. I didn't bother looking over at him. I heard his feelings through his gratitude.

"No need to thank me, Jason." I told him.

"Yeah, I do." He said and turned towards. "You protected them, when I was out here on some bullshit. You and Ma made sure that they knew me, even when I didn't know of their existence. I am grateful for that, Joel."

I looked up at him and saw how sincere he was. I gave him a half smile and nodded my head. Kymani walked backed in and gestured for us to follow him. I walked off from Jason and followed Kymel.

"Jean Pierre called in an order. He asked for Gage to do a black-out." He told us.

"Why not call and use Eliria's assassins? That is in their territory." I asked.

"I don't know, but before we give them an answer, let's run this by Fada." Kymani replied.

Eliria and her two brothers were assassins as well. They didn't have shit on us, but they were doable. Eliria ran their company and other businesses in France. They always thought that they were better than us. She asked if we wanted to battle like we were in high school or some shit. I felt that we knew our worth. We didn't have to prove anything to no one. They were all about statuses. Having their name and faces plastered everywhere. We liked being under the radar.

"Yeah, do that. We don't need no unnecessary drama." Kymel said.

The twins came running towards me with a big smile on their faces. They always did that when they wanted something. Mason stayed back and let Madison step forward. Whatever it was, Mace knew that they had a better chance with her asking.

"Mom, will it be ok if we stayed over here with Daddy. We promise to be good and not play with any weapons in the house." She said the last part for Mason. He had been told many of times to put his weapons away.

"I don't know, Lovey. Let me think about it." I told them. Madison looked like her universe was crumbling down. Mason stepped forward and grabbed her hand.

"It's ok, Maddie. Maybe next time." He told her. Jason came forward with a frown on his face.

"And why they can't?"

"I never said no, Jason." I replied.

"You didn't say yes either, Joel." He fired back.

I looked over and saw that our children were looking at us.

"Hey Lovies, give Mommy and Daddy a minute." I told them. They walked off with their heads down. Kymel and Kymani stood on the wall, watching the encounter. I glared at them. Kymel shook his head. "Now," I told them both.

"Nah, yo brothers can stay. That shit doesn't scare me." Jason said. Kymel stepped into his face and grilled him.

"Nigga you need to be." Kymel told him.

"Sho me why," Jason taunted. I saw Kymel's eyes go dark. He was about to attack him with one of his infamous blows. I got behind Kymel and hit on of his pressure points in his arm.

"FUCK, Joel. Yuh lose yuh mind." He yelled at me.

"I told you before to control yourself. If you feel like you can't, leave. We will not do this while the children around." I told him.

"Ow yuh wa wi to behave El. Dis mada fucker threatened to kill yuh wen yuh did pregnant wid di lovies. Di uhman dat him claim him loved. Mi fucking sista. Yuh wouldn't tek any uhman treating wi bad. Step back an let wi be di man dat fada teach to be. Yuh protecta." Kymel said with so much anger.

I saw the veins popping out this nigga neck, like he was on them steroids. My brother needed to release this. He needed to put his hands-on Jason to calm himself down or he was going to tear this muthafucker down. I looked over at Kymani and then at Jason.

"Lovies," I yelled out. They came running in with JoJo behind them.

"Yuh guys guh up to JoJo's room an nuh cum out." I told them. Mason grabbed both of their hands and ran up the stairs. They knew that some shit was about to go down. It wasn't the norm for me to speak Patois. Jason's family came towards us with confused looks.

"What's going on?" Jordan asked. My smile got devious. I had been waiting on that moment. Of course, Kymani was going to be upset because he didn't have anyone to fight.

"Ow bout a sparring match, ay." I told him. He smirked and nodded his head.

"Let's do it, then." Jordan replied and walked to the back of the house. Lily went upstairs with the children. She told me that she didn't want to see Jordan get hurt. I advised her that it would be best if she wasn't present.

We went out the back door and walked into the open spot. Spotlights turned on and brightened the yard up. I took my dress and tied it between my legs. Kymel started walking forward but I placed my hand on his chest. He looked down at me and saw what I knew he would see. He gently placed his hands on my face and kissed me on my nose.

"Nuh disappoint."

"Ave mi eva." I told him. Kymani came over shaking his head. I knew what he was going to say before he said it.

"Mek him feel it." He said and grabbed me to do the same thing Kymel did. I didn't care what anyone said. My brothers were better than yours. They gave me whatever I wanted and when I wanted it. I knew that Kymel's hands were itching to get on Jason, but he set that aside to let me loose for a minute.

I stepped into the circle and waited for Jordan to get in. You could see the worried look on his brother's faces, and they should be. I was ready to beat the shit out of him. Jason was staring at me. He knew what was in store for his brother. I hoped he did the right thing and stayed out of it. Because if he jumped in to help his brother, Ma-Ma was going to have to plan a triple funeral. I was sure that Joseph wouldn't stand on the side and watch my brothers kill Jason.

"No weapons," Tank called out.

"Dat a fine wid mi." I said as Jordan stepped closer to me. I dropped my head back and didn't think of my Lovies. I wanted to be in that dark place. A place where I didn't see JoJo's father, Jason's brother, Ma-Ma's son. Naw. I saw the nigga that fucked my life up.

Jordan had his shirt off, with some grey sweats. He had his dreads pulled back and started swinging practice punches. Joseph walked in

NEICY P.

the middle of us and looked at us both. He nodded his head at his brother. "Let's go." He yelled.

Finally, I thought. He put his hands up and started circling around me. Mind you, the only thing that they saw me do, was dodge a couple of punches from Jason with ease. I could hear my brothers telling me to get to work. I smiled and waited for the right opportunity. I jumped to his left, which had him of course moving to the right. I threw a right hook and connected with his jaw. Then I switched sides and hit him again. I backed up and waited for him to regroup. He put his hands up again and came at me with full force.

Jordan was trying to do what all men did when they battled against me. He tried to use his strength to overpower me. That shit wasn't going to work either. He picked me up by my waist and squeezed. I brought my elbow up and drilled it in between his neck and shoulder. It loosened up his hold just a little. Then I brought my elbow down on the top of his head. That had him dropping me. I rolled out of the way and got up. He was still dizzy from the blow to his head.

Jordan was standing with his hands on his head. I ran towards him and kicked the back of his knee. I placed my foot on his knee and back flipped off it, while hitting him under his chin, with my left knee. Jordan fell back and hit the ground hard. Jason took a step forward and so did my brothers. I kept my eyes on him as I strolled over to Jordan. I kneeled over him, then jabbed him in the throat. I started hitting him with more body shots to keep him down. Everything that I had been feeling came at me full force. The hurt and pain I suffered through. The heartbreak. The loss of a love that was hard to develop. Then, I started thinking about the times that Jason missed with the children. My blows got harder to his body. I was landing kidney shots and rib shots, since he was blocking his face. I stood over him and kicked him in the stomach, his hands came down and I punched him in the face, knocking his ass out. He was going to suffer just like I did.

I heard Ma-Ma call out my name. I looked up at her with an agitated expression. That was one of the reasons why I worked alone.

THE WAY TO A KILLER'S HEART 2

I didn't like being interrupted. JJ grabbed Ma-Ma and placed her behind, while the other men stepped forward. Tee Glen walked back to where Ma-Ma was standing. I looked down at an unconscious Jordan. He was breathing, barely. But, hey that was my intentions. I glared up and saw that Jason was ready for battle. Kymel and Kymani came and stood by my side. "Now," Kymel asked.

"Yea bredda. Now." I whispered.

Kymel went straight for Jason.

"No, get my baby." Ma-Ma hollered out.

"Take the women in the house, Tristan." JJ yelled and came after Kymani, with Tank. Kymani smiled and rotated his shoulders.

"A lil workout neva hurt anyone." He said right before Tank swung at him. Tristan picked Ma-Ma up and carried her to the house with Tee Glen watching. I knew that she wasn't going to leave. She pulled out her gun and waited to see how everything was going to turn out.

I sat on the ground, in front of Jordan's body and watched. Jason and Kymel was going blow for blow. Tank and JJ was getting some punches in on Kymani, but that shit wasn't going to last. Kymani was toying with them. He didn't have anything against the men, but I knew that he respected them more for fighting with their family.

I looked over at Jason and he was doing well. Kymel swung and Jason ducked hitting him in the ribs. Jason swung again and Kymel caught his arm. He spun Jason around and put him in a sleeper. Jason started elbowing Kymel's side but just like the punch before, it didn't faze him at all. JJ saw how Kymel had Jason. He went over and punched Kymel in the face. Kymel dropped Jason and went at JJ hard. Kymani hit Tank with a paralyzing punch to the chest. Tank went down clutching his chest. Tee Glen raised her gun up to shoot at Kymani.

I quickly jumped up and rolled to Kymani. I pulled his knife from the strap around his ankle and threw it at her. The gun flew out her hand. I ran to where the gun was and picked it up. I raised it and shot out the spotlights that were in the yard. Everything went black. We already had the advantage because of the skills we possessed. But, the

NEICY P.

dark was something we craved. We were still able to see as if the lights were still on.

I heard a door open and slammed shut. I turned and continued to watch the fight before the person that was coming behind me stopped it. He didn't like Jason nor Jordan, but he promised Pops that he was going to watch over him. Emergency lights came on and the men were still fighting. My father stood next to me and shook his head.

"I thought you guys were here for the children."

"We did. Tings change." I said. He looked over at me and saw the blood on my hands. He looked back at the yard and saw that Jordan was on the ground along with Tank.

"El," Papa called out to me.

"Him nuh dead." I whispered.

"Gud, now stop dis shit." He said and walked back to the house. He asked Tee Glen to follow him and that I was going to take care of everything. Poppa knew that I had a better chance with stopping them then he did. That was why he didn't try. I took a deep breath and walked towards the men. All of this shit was happening because my duck ass fell in love with Jason. My brothers warned me about niggas like that. They told me that they couldn't be trusted. I thought that they were saying that to keep me away from the men in this game. But all along they were being honest. Kymel and Kymani were right to feel the way they felt about Jason. If he was the man that I needed him to be, then he would have been there when I needed him. Jordan wasn't the blame for this shit. Jason was.

I thought about the love and the time I wasted on his punk ass. I tried to make him see that there was more to life than the next kill. And the ones that suffered the most was my children. I had to explain to them that their father was ill and couldn't see them yet. I made excuses for his actions and I was done with it.

"Bruddas, dat is enough." I told them. Kymani pushed off JJ and stood back with his hands up. They both had small injuries that could be fixed. Kymel and Jason didn't stop. Kymani walked over to them and yelled for them to stop. That didn't work.

"Mel, please stop." I said softly. They both stopped and looked at me.

"El, what's wrong?" Mel asked walking towards me. Kymani reached me first and placed his hand on my face. He stared down at me and wiped my eyes. Tears. I didn't know I was crying. I held them tears in for years. Jason began to walk towards me, while JJ went and checked on his brother and Tank.

"Mani, can you please help JJ with them. After that we can go." I told him. "The children can stay here with you. I'll come and pick them up tomorrow." I told him and walked off with Mel holding my hand. I had never felt so vulnerable before in my life. I felt weak and lost. And for the first time, I felt out of control. Jason called out my name, but I ignored him. I went back into the house and saw Ma-Ma and Tee Glen sitting at the table with Poppa. Tristan ran out the door to check on his brother.

Tee Glen and Ma-Ma was staring at me like they wanted to go a round with me. Poppa saw me and walked towards me. He grabbed my shoulders and pulled me to him.

"What's wrong Butterfly?" He asked. I couldn't talk. I didn't want him to think that this was something that I couldn't handle. I shook my head and tried to walk away. His grip became tight and he asked me again. I didn't answer. I felt my anxiety rise. I felt like I was in a box, with no place to go. I…I just…I just wanted to scream.

Jason came in the house and saw my face. Without saying anything to anyone, he scooped me up and carried me to a car outside. I heard my father tell Kymel to stand down. He knew that Jason wouldn't hurt me. Jason opened the door and placed me in. I didn't know why I stayed in there. I was trying to get away from him. He jumped in the driver seat and peeled off. No music. No conversation. Nothing.

It wasn't how I wanted our day to end. He pulled up to this theater. He got out and came around to open the door for me. I sat there not understanding why he brought me here. When he saw that I wasn't going to move, he reached in and picked me up out of my seat. He opened the door and placed me on my feet when we got in. He took my hand and walked me into one off the doors. It was a big ass theater with a stage. It was missing the big screen.

Jason lifted me up and placed me on top of the stage. He took a step back and sat in the front seat. I looked around at the huge open space. I sat on the floor with my eyes closed, grabbed my knees, and started rocking. We all had our days. The day when you feel like it was you against the world. You started thinking about all the decisions you had made and how it affected the ones around you. I didn't regret my children, not one bit. I just regretted their father. Many women felt this way about their no-good ass baby daddies.

I felt my anxiety leaving and the need to scream vanished. The rocking stopped, and I let my legs fall. When I opened my eyes, Jason was staring at me. I didn't want to acknowledge the fact that he knew exactly what I needed. I stood up and jumped off the stage. I began to walk back to the door, but Jason grabbed my arm.

"Are you feeling better?" He asked, looking like his normal self. His eye and mouth was swollen.

"I'm fine." I told him and pulled my arm out of his hand. "I'll see you on tomorrow." I continued and walked up the aisle. He came behind me and yanked my arm again. This time I turned and swung on his ass, connecting with his jaw. "Leave me the fuck alone Jason. Just go and be with our children. Make up the time that y'all lost." I said to him.

He just looked at me. "Are you good, Joel?" He ignored and asked me again. I didn't know what type of answer he was looking for. We weren't on good terms to discuss feelings and shit. I wanted to leave this place and call Tyja. My best friend was able to make sense out of anything. I knew she was going to be mad, when I tell her how I fucked Jordan up. She wanted to be there for that. Tyja really wanted to come and see JJ. She missed him so much, but she also hated that JJ didn't try and talk to Jason after Pops died. She blamed JJ and I blame Jordan. Well, she got that one right.

"I am not your concern. The ones that you need to worry about is at your parents' home." I answered. I stood my ground this time because if his ass grabbed my arm again, I was going to go batshit crazy on his ass. No bullshit.

"Let it go, El." He said to me and it felt like I was experiencing Deja-vu. This was the same shit I told him to do when we were in New Orleans. In this situation, he had no right.

"Save that shit fa someone that need it. Go check on our children." I told him and left the theater. I walked up the street thinking of some kills I could have made to get my mind off his silly ass. Lord knows I needed it.

JORDAN

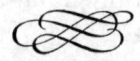

It had been a week since the battle, and my body was still aching. Joel fucked me up. I couldn't lie about that. I didn't know how skillful she really was. Lily tried to nurse me back to health. My body was bruised up and I felt like it was hard to breathe at times. I never had asthma before, but now it seemed like I needed an asthma pump after climbing stairs. The shit was crazy.

Joel came to the house and gave Lily some herbs and medicine that they used. I took some on yesterday and was feeling much better than before. I was sitting going over some calls with our managers. JJ had been taking care of the two warehouses where our merchandise was. Jason had been spending some much-needed time with his children. It was amazing how much they looked like JoJo.

Ma-Ma was having a blast with all her grandchildren under one roof. She got up and cooked breakfast, then lunch, and prepped for dinner. Madison helped her in the kitchen with Lily. Mason and JoJo played on their video games, with Jason watching over them. You were able to see how much he was changing already. Lily and I thought that it would be best if JoJo was homeschooled. When JoJo was busy with his lesson, the twins were doing theirs on the computer with their online teachers. They were extremely smart children. After they finished their lesson, they taught JoJo whatever they learned. JoJo asked us if it was okay for him to learn a different language. We were more than okay with that.

After talking to all the managers, I got up and went into the kitchen. Ma was in there by herself rolling up some meatballs. "They abandoned you." I asked her, after kissing her on the cheek.

"Lily said that she was feeling tired. Madison walked her up the stairs to make sure she gets in the bed. That little girl is more possessive as you are over Lily." She answered.

"Yeah, she is. Madison is a small version of Joel." I said and sat at the table. Ma washed her hands and came sat down with me.

"How are you feeling?" Ma asked.

"I am feeling much better. I still gotta talk to Jason and make shit with us right again." I replied.

"Yeah, I think that he is in a better mindset to accept your apology." She said to me.

"I first want to apologize to you, Ma. I am sorry that I let you and Pops down. Y'all raised me better than that. I just wanted us to have it all. We deserve that. You and Pops worked so hard to put us ahead of the game and to keep us on top. I felt that we were sharing that spot with people that didn't put in the demanding work like y'all did. I watched as the children of the Stand used our name to gain respect and shit from other vendors. It made me mad and my anger caused Pops' death.

I wish I could take back all the pain and grief that I caused you, Ma. That I caused this family. I want my brothers to trust me again and I am willing to do whatever it takes for that to happen. If I gotta step down from being the leader of the Davis crew, so be it." I confessed to her. I had been thinking about stepping down for a while now. The decision I had made had been for my own selfish reasons.

"I forgave you a long time ago, Jordan. But you don't have to step down to show us that you are sorry. You just have to involve your brothers more. Don't assume that they want the same thing as you. You all are different but if you compromise and keep everybody's best interest in mind, the decision would be easier to make. Trust is hard to gain when you lose it the way that you did. You can't force them to forgive you. You have to wait until they are ready." Ma told me. And for the first time I listened to understand and not to respond. Ma was always right when it came to shit like this. I had to take the first step and hoped that my brothers forgave me.

"Grandma, are you finish yet." Madison walked in and asked.

"Almost, suga. Do you want to help?" Ma asked her while getting up. She walked to the island and continued rolling the meatballs.

"Sure. I have to wash my hands first." She responded. She looked over to me and smiled. "Uncle Jo, are you going to help us?" She asked me. I stood, picked her up, and took her to sink to wash her hands.

"No, Princess. I can't roll meatballs like you and your Grandma." I told her.

"It doesn't take a genius to roll meatballs Uncle Jo. If you have other things to do, I'll understand." Madison said so sweetly. Ma laughed and shook her head.

"Ok, smarty. I need to talk to your father and Uncle JJ about some stuff." I told her. I placed her on the kitchen island, next to Ma. Madison grabbed my face and kissed me on the cheek.

"Uncle JJ just got back. He is upstairs playing the game with Daddy." She told me. I smiled down at her and tugged her ponytail.

"Thank you." I told her and went upstairs to talk to my brothers.

I opened the door to the game room and saw that Jason and JJ were playing a basketball game. JoJo and Mason were cheering them on. JJ had the Thunder and Jason had the Warriors. JJ was beating Jason by two points with only thirteen seconds on the clock. Curry was coming down with the ball and shot a half-court shot.

"OOHHHHH!" Mason and JoJo yelled out when the shot went in.

"Man, you cheated. You can't be using Curry like that, bruh." JJ said and dropped the game controller on the floor.

"Take yo lost like a man, bruh." Jason told him. Mason walked over to him and gave him a dap.

"That was awesome Dad. I knew he didn't have a chance when he sat down." Mason told him. JJ looked over at him with a frown on his face.

"Stop boosting him up." JJ told him and got up. JoJo and Mason picked the controllers up and started playing the game.

"Hey, can I holla at y'all for a minute." I asked Jason and JJ. JJ walked out the door, while Jason sat in the chair behind the boys.

"I don't want to talk about nothing right now, Jo. Let me stay in my happy place, bruh." Jason said to me.

"J, it will only take a couple of minutes. I really need to talk to you." I told him.

It was different talking to my mother about feelings and shit. But, it was a totally different story when you talk about that type of shit with your brothers. Jason looked up at me with a warning.

"I'll be right back, boys." He whispered to them. Mason paused the game and looked back at his father. Jason got up and followed JJ out the door. I turned to walk behind him when Mason stopped me.

"Hey, Unc." He called out.

"What's up nephew?" I said, looking back at him.

"Can you please make sure that my Daddy come back?" He asked me.

I nodded my head and walked out the door. I went downstairs into the office, where they were waiting. JJ was at the bar fixing us all a drink. Jason sat across the room. I knew he was trying to keep his distance from me. I sat and waited for JJ to finish. When he passed me my drink and sat in front the desk, I took the drink and cleared my throat.

"I had been thinking a lot lately, about the shit that I started years back. I was selfish and didn't really listen to what everyone had to say. I was wrong to think that I had the final say in everything that was supposed to be for us, together. I am ready to listen and suffer any of the consequences to make us right again. We all knew that this was something that our parents wanted. What I'm trying to say is, that... I'm sorry. I'm sorry for all the pain that I caused the family." I said.

I stood and walked in Jason's direction. He was staring at me with dark eyes. I didn't let that stop me. "Jason, I know that it's going to take some time for me to regain the trust and the love you had for me. I just want you to know that I am sorry for blaming you for Pops' death. I'm sorry that you didn't see your children brought into this world. Man, I'm sorry for everything." I continued.

I wasn't looking for them to say anything back. I just wanted them to hear me out. I started walking towards the door and stopped when JJ started talking.

"Jo, bruh. We both been telling you how selfish you were, and you made it seem like we were wrong. You just don't know how that shit made me felt. I can't speak for Jason, but you made it seem like we were under you. You ran around this bitch barking orders out and didn't bother to ask our opinion on shit. I'm happy that you came to your senses and apologized. Cause I was going to fuck you up next." He told me and stood up. He gave me a brotherly hug and smacked me on my back. JJ and I had our issues. But, it wasn't like the ones that me and Jason had. JJ stepped back and looked at Jason. I waited to see what he was going to say.

Jason rubbed his hand down his face and stood. He walked over to us and motioned for us to get out of the way. I moved to the side and let him pass. He stopped in the doorway and spoke.

"Give me some time Jo." He told me and walked back upstairs. JJ smiled at me and went to the kitchen. I knew that it will be hard moving forward, but at least we were moving in the right direction.

JASON

Yeah, that nigga apologized but I didn't want to hear that shit. Pops was gone, and I lost Joel behind Jordan's bullshit. That nigga was going to have to do more than apologize for me to get back what I lost. When Jo started talking, I wanted to remove that fool's tongue out of his mouth. It took Joel to beat his ass to see shit for what they really were.

I went back upstairs and watched Mason and JoJo play the game. I didn't do much this past week but spend time with my children. I found out that my babies were five going on twenty. Their birthday was the same as my father, July 15. They spoke several different languages. We saw the math that they were doing and JJ's stupid ass walked off.

"I know they bet not need help with that shit. I haven't done problems like that in a while. I'll be fucked if I let them make me travel down that memory lane." He said.

I was amazed at how much they knew. I caught them talking in another language during dinner. I looked over at everyone's expression and I was happy to see the looks on their faces. Joel told me that she graduated two years early from high school and college. She was raising our children to be little geniuses. I asked them about their knowledge on weapons and they got excited. When baby girl told me that she can make a grown man cry, I believed her. Hell, look who her father was. Fuck that, look who her mother was. Mason's tablet started blinking. He looked over at it and saw that it was his Mom. He swiped to answer it.

"Hello, Ma. How are you doing today?" He asked while looking down at the screen.

"I am doing well, son. How are you? Are you misbehaving over there?" She asked.

"I am also doing well, Ma. I have been on my best behavior. Madison is in the kitchen cooking with Grandma. Daddy and JoJo is here playing the game with me." He told her.

"That is good, Lovey. I was just calling checking up on you two. I'll pick you guys up on Thursday, ok." She said.

"Ok, that's cool Mommy. Can JoJo come with us? He is going to be all alone with these adults. Aunt Lily can't really do much with him because she is always tired. Uncle Jo is going back to work soon, and Daddy is going to be busy. Please Ma." Mason begged.

"Sure, baby. You know that I don't have a problem with JoJo coming over. He would have to ask his parents first." She replied.

"Yes," JoJo said and ran off to get his parents' permission.

"You are the best. I love you." He told her with a loving expression.

"I love you, more." She replied.

"Not today," he whispered. He was about to hang up.

"Hey, let me talk to your Mom right quick." I asked and reached for his tablet. He gave it to me and I saw Joel on the other end. She had her hair straight and no make-up, just the way I liked it.

"Jason," she said dryly.

"Beautiful," I told her. She rolled her eyes at my compliment.

"What do you want?" She asked me. I was stunned by her beauty. My baby girl looked just like her. "I was about to take the kids out for lunch. Do you want to join us?" I lied.

"No, bye." She said. Mason jumped up and stood next to me.

"Mommy please. I get to take the picture that I wanted for my wallpaper." He asked her.

She smiled over at him and shook her head. "Ok, baby. Mommy will see you in twenty minutes." Her smile dropped when she looked over at me. "Bye," she said with a lot of attitude and hung up. Mason shook his head and sighed.

"Dad, you have no game. It's alright, though. I have your back. I'll tell Madison that we are trying to get you back together with Mom." He said and picked up the controller.

"Boy, I don't need your help." I told him.

He looked at me and smiled. "Sure, you don't," he said and continued playing the game. JoJo came back in the room.

"She said yes."

"Cool. You know you don't have to pack. We shopped for you three weeks ago." Mason told him.

"Good looking out." JoJo said and picked the other controller up and started playing with him. I looked down at these two boys and saw me and my brothers when we were young. Mason looked out for JoJo like he was his brother. I got up and went downstairs to tell Madison that we were going out with her Mom. When I got in the kitchen, Ma and Madison were cleaning.

"Hey baby girl, do you want to go to lunch with Mason and me? Your Mom is coming with us." I asked her. The smile that spread across her face was priceless.

"Yes. Daddy. I am going to change before Mommy get here." She said and ran out of the kitchen.

"That's my girl, right there." Ma said. "I'm proud of you, son."

"Thanks, Ma. I need to change too. Let me know when Joel gets here." I said.

* * *

"Mom, can I get my hair cut." Mason asked Joel, as we sat and ate our dessert. Joel looked at him with a confused expression. "Why do you want your hair cut, Mason."

"I want to look like my Dad." He whispered. Joel looked over at me with a smile.

"Ask your father, son? Maybe he could take you to his barber." She answered. Mason looked back at me with bright eyes. I couldn't do nothing but smile, while he waited for my answer.

"Whatever you want, man." I told him.

Madison started touching his hair and told him how much she was going to miss it. I looked over at Joel and whispered, "Thank you." She smirked at me and shook her head. I knew she wanted to say more but didn't want to discuss whatever in front of the children. My phone started vibrating and it was Sierra. She had been calling me non-stop over the week. She left me voice and text messages on my phone. I really didn't have time for her ass now. I had a lot to make up with my children. Joel started ringing. She pulled it out, looked at it, and excused herself from the table.

I couldn't help but wonder who was on the other end. "Don't worry about it Daddy. It's either Uncle Mel or Uncle Mani." Madison told me.

"And, how do you know that?" I asked.

"Because Mommy still loves you. She used to leave the house and go see you to take pictures for us. I caught her a couple of times looking at the pictures when we were supposed to be sleeping. Grandma says when someone looks like that at someone else that means that they love them." She explained while eating her ice cream. *Ok*, I thought.

Joel came back in with a smile on her face. "Ok, lovies. It's time for us to go. Go and wash your hands." Mason took Madison's hand and walked her to the bathroom. We weren't worried about no one getting to them because they had their own strict guards. When they were gone, Joel began to speak. "I have to go. We have to deal with the family of the Stand members. They are thinking that it was Leng people that did it. Greg and Sean's shipments had been short. They warned them many of times about it.

The night that we came to the warehouse, some of Leng people were there. They wanted to kill everybody in attendance. Mani didn't really feel like arguing with them, so he killed two of their men. Leng forgave us for it only if we finished the Stand off. We told him that it was going to be done. He also told us that he and his organization would take the fall for it. But you know my work is my work. I would never let another man take credit for my work. Some of the men are meeting at three on Fifth Street. What are you guys going to do?" She said.

"You know I rather for us to kill them all but it's not my call. I'll talk to my brothers and see what they want to do." I told her. She nodded her head and started texting on her phone. While the kids were still washing their hands, I decided to ask her about that smirk. "Hey what was all that about, with Mason's haircut? I said thank you."

"I didn't do that for you, Jason. I did it for Mason. He has been looking for this moment to bond with you for a long time. I didn't want to ruin that for him. Just like I know that Marquel told you I didn't want them with them weapons yet. And you still got them." She said with an attitude.

"Come on, Joel. You were training my kids to be killers, without my consent. They have been handling weapons, without my consent. You have had made many choices for our children, without my consent. I choose one thing for them and it's a problem." I asked her. I wasn't trying to be confrontational. I just wanted her to see where I was coming from.

She sighed and looked over at me. "When we were in New Orleans, we talked about what we wanted for our kids, if we had any. You said, that you wanted them to train as soon as they were able to walk. I honored your wishes. Everything that I have done for the children, was done with you in mind." She said and walked to the sink with the children. I didn't know what to say after that. Clearly, if we were together they would be doing the same thing that they had been doing.

I walked out the door and called Jordan. "What's up, J?" He answered.

"Aye, Joel brothers just intercepted a message that some of the family members are looking for answers. Leng was talking about taking the fall for it, but Callum is not with that shit. The men are meeting up at three." I told him.

"Where," He sounded like he was getting in his car.

"On Fifth Street." I replied.

"Cool, we can meet up on Second Street at Caps. I will call JJ and tell him what is going on. Tank and Tristan will be there, too." He said and hung up the phone. I turned to see what was taking Joel and the children so long, when Sierra and Tasha walked up. This was the shit I didn't have time for.

"So, I have been calling you over a week now, and you still haven't called back yet. You are that mad at me." Sierra said with her hands on her hip.

"Sierra, you know when I say something, I mean it. I don't play that going through my phone type of shit. I wasn't yo man and you weren't my girl. We fucked a lot and that's all it was. Don't make a fool out yourself and try to cause a scene." I told her and walked past her.

"We did more than fuck, Jason. So, don't try to play me, because you found out that some random chick had your kids and you didn't want to tell me. I had every right to react the way I did when I been down for you." She said with anger.

"Go ahead with that shit. You were down for the title and that was it. We didn't go out. I didn't buy you gifts or offer you shit. Even when yo Pops tried to hook something up more between us, I turned that shit down quick. If closure is what you are looking for, well here it is. It's over. Stop calling and texting me." I told her.

"Bitch, I know you ain't gon' let that nigga shine on you like that. You better call your brothers so that they can deal with him." Tasha said. She was the typical *"ain't got shit"* friend. The fake hair, nails, body, teeth, and anything else that hoe could have bought. Sierra always let Tasha gas her ass up to do stupid shit. That was another reason why I didn't see myself with her. She wasn't her own woman and that shit drove me.

"Call yo punk ass brothers down here if you want. Whatever happens to them, will be your fault. That you do know." I told her.

"Fuck you, Jason. You ain't gon' touch my fucking brothers. And I can't wait 'til they come down here. They gon' fuck you up and take all of your shit." She screamed.

"Is there a problem?" I heard Joel ask. Sierra looked over my shoulder and saw her and my children by her side.

"Oh, you over here trying to play Daddy to some children that you don't even know is yours. You are a true duck." Sierra said out loud. Tasha started laughing all ugly. Madison came stood next to me and grabbed my hand. She tugged at it while looking up at me.

"Daddy, can we go now." She said.

"Uh, lil girl. Go over there by your mother. It looks like you don't understand when two adults are speaking, you don't interrupt." Sierra said to Madison.

I took a step away from Madison and got in Sierra's face. I didn't want my daughter to see me get out of character with a woman, but the way she talked to her had my blood heated. Madison came to my side and grabbed my hand again.

"Just ignore her, Daddy." She said softly. Baby girl didn't let Sierra's words get to her. She had patience that I couldn't pay to have. I still was grilling her. My hands were twitching to get around this hoe neck.

Sierra smiled at me like she won. "Trust and believe me when I say that you just fucked up."

Madison dropped my hand and stepped forward. The pretty little girl I usually see was gone and lil Gage had taken her place. "Excuse mi. Yuh just threatened mi fada." She told Sierra. Her voice got cold and deadly. Joel heard what Madison said and walked over to us.

"Madison," Joel asked. Madison shook her head and that had Joel ready to rip Sierra and Tasha's head off. "Is there a problem." She asked again, looking directly at me. I picked my lil monster up and shook my head no.

"Oh, there is a problem. I had been with Jason for almost three years. How come he just hearing about these kids." Sierra spoke out. Joel kept her eyes on me and reached for a seething Madison.

"Handle this, before I do." She said and walked off ignoring Sierra.

Madison was still glaring at Sierra with a menacing look. The look that Joel had given Jo many times. I knew that Sierra just sealed her faith and that it would be Madison to take her life. I didn't have anything to say to Sierra after that. I turned and walked off behind my family.

SIERRA

"Oh, he done fucked up." I told Tasha and pulled out my phone.

"Gurl, you should've reached over him and beat the shit out of that woman." Tasha said. We watched as they pulled off in his Escalade. Before they took off, I took pictures of the chick and the children. I knew that my brothers were going to need them. I told Tasha that I was going to talk to her later. I didn't feel like being bothered after seeing that shit. We hugged and went our separate ways. I was beyond livid. Jason was out here being a family man, while I was waiting on him to call me back. I wasn't going to let his ugly ass baby mama come in between us. I should go to his condo and wait for him. I needed to talk to him alone. I dialed his number again and this time it went straight to voicemail. I hung up and dialed again. Nothing. I was getting frustrated. I called my brother to tell him what happened.

"What's up, Cici?" Alan answered.

"Jason have been cheating on me. He is walking around flaunting his family in my face. I had been calling him for a week, after he put me out of his condo. Al, it is so embarrassing." I told him. I didn't want to admit how hurt I was. I was in love with him. I would have waited for him to feel the same way. I felt the tears building up. I didn't want

Tasha to see me cry. She was going to clown me and tell everyone how sprung I was behind Jason.

"Don't worry sis. We will take care of Jason." Alan responded.

"No, I don't want you to take care of Jason. Get rid of his baby mama. See if you can send some of the assassins after her and the children." I demanded.

"Damn, sis. You want to kill the children too." Alan laughed. "The children didn't do you nothing. I wouldn't mind killing off the woman, but I ain't killing no kids."

"UGH, don't laugh at me Al. I am serious. I don't think he feels anything for the children's mother. If we killed all three of them, Jason would lose his shit." I suggested.

"I'll talk to Brandon and Dad about this or you can come home and talk to them. It's been a minute since we had seen you. It would be a great surprise for him." Alan said.

"Yeah, you right. Can you send the jet, please?" I asked, while jumping into my car.

"I gotcha," he said and hung up. I knew that it was going to take some time to get the jet ready, so I pulled up at his condo. I sat and waited for him in the parking lot. When he didn't show up, I turned off the car and went into his building. The older woman was sitting there watching some daytime show on her TV. I approached the desk and asked for the key.

"Excuse me, can I have the key to the top floor."

She looked at me over her big rim glasses. "Mr. Davis don't want you in his condo. Matter fact you are not allowed in this building."

"What are you talking about? I just saw him an hour ago. He told me to meet him in the condo." I lied. She picked up the phone and dialed his number and put him on speakerphone. He answered it on the third ring.

"Yes, Ms. Gladys."

"That woman is here talking about you told her to wait in your condo." She said with disgust.

"Don't worry. Buzz Butch, he already knows what to do." He said with laughing children in the background. The old bitch hung up with a smile on her face and continued watching TV. I didn't know who Butch was, but I wasn't going to sit here and get embarrassed by getting thrown out of the building. I walked out of there and jumped back into my car. I drove to our private airstrip and waited for the jet to arrive. After it landed, I got out my car and walked towards it. It opened, and my dad and brothers were walking down the stairs.

I ran into my Dad's open arms. "Alan told me that you were having some problems out here. Let's go and grab something to eat and talk about these problems." He told me.

Jordan

"How do y'all want to handle this?" I asked my brothers. We were sitting in the office at Caps discussing what we wanted to do with the other family members of the stand.

"We can kill them all." Jason said nonchalantly.

"I'm down for that, but how would that affect our businesses? Derrick and Sean were our partners with the Distributors. Greg's family have half of the police station on his payroll along with a couple of FBI agents. If we kill them, we have to kill everybody that is associated with them." JJ said. I nodded my head agreeing with him.

"And that is going to take some time. Lily is about to give birth to Jeramiah any day now. I don't want to put her in any more danger." I told them.

"Aight. Well, what can we do? Cause I don't want to wait for them bitches to come after us." Jason said. "But, Joel said that they will take the fall for it. I'm not cool with pointing the finger at my woman." He continued and shook his head. That was not an option at all.

"When Joel became your woman again." I asked him. I didn't know if he was going to respond or not. I just threw that out there to see if he did. He looked at me and smiled.

"She never stopped being my woman. Joel will always have my heart. Whether she want it or not." He whispered. The office phone rang and broke the brief silence that we shared. I picked it up and answered.

"Jordan."

"Jordan, this is Vince, Sean's nephew. Do you have a minute?" He asked.

"Yeah, what's up?" I told him and put him on speaker.

"Before my uncle left the house, he told my Aunt that he was meeting with some of the members of the Stand. He didn't say your name because he told us that you and your family was dealing with a family emergency. We wanted to know if you heard anything about the murders. Do you know if the Stand had problems with anyone?" He asked.

"No, we weren't having problems with anyone that I know of. Did your Uncle tell you what kind of family emergency we had?" I asked curiously.

"He said that someone killed your wife and child. I'm sorry for your loss. I didn't want to call you with this because I knew that your family must be in a lot of pain. We weren't coming up with nothing. I thought that maybe you guys knew something." He answered. I looked over at my brothers. Those muthafuckers were claiming that my family died even before the assassins came after them. I wished that Joel and her brothers would have let us handle them.

"You were misinformed. My sister and nephew are alive and well. Whatever your uncle had planned, he didn't want to involve us. Go, and talk to Leng. He is waiting on your call." Jason said and hung up.

"Yo, Joel is going to fuck you up." JJ said.

"She could do whatever she wants. I am not putting her or her brothers in this shit." He said and walked out of the office. JJ looked over at me with a stunned expression.

"Look, bruh. I love y'all with everything in me. But I'm telling you this right now, I ain't fighting Shadow or Reap again, nigga. That muthafucker had me coughing up blood for three days. I'm shooting their asses. Fuck that." JJ said.

He was sitting there whining about Shadow and Reaper. Joel

fucked me up. I was still limping from the shots she gave me. Tank and Tristan walked in while we were talking.

"Hey, what are y'all doing for the rest of the day?" Tank asked.

"Lily wanted to Netflix and chill." I told them.

"Damn, her ass already pregnant. How many kids y'all trying to have anyway?" Tristan asked, while JJ and Tank laughed at his previous comment.

"This is the last one, man. I was hoping for a girl, but I'll be happy with two boys. Jason is going to have to share Madison." I told them. They all nodded their head in agreement. JJ jumped up with a big ass smile on his face.

"Oh yeah, ya bitch you. You told my niece that you were going to be her sparring partner today. Come on, nigga. Let's go. Don't be trying to get out of it either." JJ said walking out of the door. We all followed him out. We had to see baby Gage in action. Jason was on the phone when we came out.

"What's going on?" Jason asked hanging up the phone.

"Tristan here, volunteered to be Madison's sparring partner." Tank said squeezing Tristan shoulder. Jason looked over at Tristan with a deadly look and then smiled.

"Let's go." He said and jumped in his car with JJ.

We all drove like we were on *Fast and the Furious* to the house. When we got in the house, Madison was already out in the back stretching with Mason. "Uncle Tristan, you're late." She said in the sweetest voice. Tristan went and picked her up and kissed her on the cheek.

"I'm sorry, Princess. Your Uncle Jo called a meeting that I had to attend to." He said and put her down.

"Well I guess I can't be mad at you then. Are you ready? Do you need to stretch?" She asked him.

"No, pretty girl. I'm ready."

"Ok," she said and took some steps away from him.

Joel walked out with her brothers behind her. We watched as the sweet little girl we knew face changed like she was a predator. Tristan didn't know how to attack a little girl. None of us did. Tristan looked back at us for some type of instructions. Tank hunched his shoulders. Tristan turned towards Madison and tried to grab her. She sidestepped him and kicked the side of his knee.

"Ahh, shit." Tristan said and went down grabbing his knee. Shadow shook his head and walked forward.

"Get yo weak ass out here." He said and waited for Tristan to roll out of the way. Shadow went at Madison full force. He swung at her and she danced gracefully around him. When she did hit him, it was in places that I wouldn't think to hit anyone. Joel smiled at her daughter. Reaper laughed out loud with every hit. We didn't understand until we saw that Shadow started moving slower. It looked like Madison had the upper hand, but Shadow caught her by her ponytail and threw her to the ground. We all stepped forward. Joel and Reaper had to grab Jason to keep him from going out there.

Madison got up and had a cut above her eye. "Your enemy is not going to care that you are a little girl, Madison. They are going to use whatever they can, to take you out." He grilled her. Madison closed her eyes and opened them with determination. She got into a fighting stance and waited for Shadow to attack her. He moved forward and tried to hit her again. Only this time Madison ducked, and Mason came out of nowhere and kicked him in the chest with both feet. Mason fell on the ground and jumped up in a fighting stance.

"Holy shit, nigga. Did you see that? They look like Crouching Tiger out there." JJ yelled out.

Jason was now standing without anyone holding him back. He watched as his children kicked their Uncle ass, with moves that had all of us taking notes. By the time they were done, Shadow was out of breath and couldn't move. Mason walked over to his sister and looked at the cut over her eye.

"Are you ok, sis?" He asked.

"Yeah, I'm fine. I shouldn't have taken my eyes off him. That was totally my fault. It won't happen again, though. That is a promise." She said walking towards us, with her brother.

"Where y'all learn how to fight like that?" Tank asked them.

"From my mother's Parrain. He knew that, in hand to hand combat, our punches won't do the damage that a grown-up would do. Once we learned the anatomy of the body, he taught us all the pressure points that would weaken our opponents. That way, we could grab an object to finish them off with." Mason explained. Jason was examining Madison's face. She pushed his hand away. "I am fine Daddy. It's just a scratch that will heal over time. It's no big deal." She told him and walked into the house. Jason looked over at Joel with a frown.

"I don't like that shit, Joel. For Mason yeah, it's understandable. But not for my little girl." He said shaking his head.

"You can't get all upset because she didn't want you babying her. She is tough, just like us." She said and walked into the house after Madison. Shadow finally got up and looked down at Mason. Mason looked at him like he was taller than his uncle. Shadow stuck his hand out to shake his nephew's hand.

"Gud job, mi boi." He told him.

"Thanks, Unc." He said with a smile. Mason looked back at his father. "What did you think Dad?" Jason walked over to him and scooped him up.

"You were great, man. I'm proud of you." He told him. Mason hugged his father tightly, before Jason put him down. Mason ran into the house to make sure his sister was alright.

"We got a call from Greg's nephew earlier. He asked us what we know." I told them.

Shadow stretched out the pain that the children inflicted on him. "Did you tell them that we did it?"

"No," Jason stepped in and answered. "I told them that it was Leng and his crew."

Shadow and Reaper looked over at Jason with wide eyes. "You gave someone else the credit for Gage work." Reaper said and took a step back.

"I'll deal with whatever consequences behind that. I didn't want nobody coming after her behind our shit." Jason said. Shadow and Reaper looked at each other and smiled. Reaper walked forward and held his hand out. Jason looked at, before shaking it. Shadow did the same.

"Welcome to the family, man." They told him. "I just hope you live long enough to see the next day. She is going to be pissed when you tell her." Shadow told him.

Joel walked out with Lily. "Tell me what." She asked us.

I took Lily's hand and walked right back in the house. That was a conversation I didn't want to get involved with. I was just getting back good with both of them. I'll be damn if I had to choose a side. I sat Lily down and went to fix her something to eat. I didn't have to ask if she was hungry, because her ass was always eating. Even when she was full. I sat a plate of spaghetti with meatballs, and some fresh garlic bread in front of her.

"Thank you, babe." She told me. I kissed her on them candy tasting lips and bricked up quick. She smiled up at me. "After I feed your little man, then I could feed you." She whispered, grabbing at my stick.

"Well, let me get another one of those to hold me down." I asked and leaned in for another kiss. That time, I slipped my tongue into her mouth. She moaned out and grabbed my face. I knew she couldn't resist my tongue. She was addicted to me like I was to her. We had to cross a lot of bridges to get where we were right now. But the love I had for her had never changed. She was still the only woman I wanted to see when I woke up in the morning and rest with at night. She got up from the table and took my hand. She led me to the downstairs bathroom and locked it. She sat on the toilet and pulled me to her. Lily pulled my man out of my pants and licked the tip. I knew I had to be quiet because of the children and the other guests. The shit was going to be hard to do. Especially when she wrapped her wet mouth around the rim of it.

"Damn, Lily. Don't tease your man like that." I groaned out and grabbed her head. She relaxed her throat and let me slide in with no resistance from her hands. "Mm, baby. Do what I know only you could do?" I told her.

She wrapped her tongue around me and began to give me the best head ever. She started making that slurping sound and humming on my shit. I had to turn the vent on in the bathroom to drown out the sounds. She tightened her cheeks up and that was my undoing. I spilled the good shit all down her throat.

Lily let my stick out of her mouth with a little pop. She got up and turned around. She raised her dress up and bent down. Her ass was nice and plump from the pregnancy. Her ass was wet from giving me head. I saw how wet she was through her panties. I pulled them down and kneeled before her. I licked my other favorite set of lips with my thick tongue.

"Oh, Jordan. Give me that dick Jordan. Please." She begged. She thought her ass was slick. Lily knew if I would have pulled her pearl in my mouth, she was going to bust all over my face. I shook my head and grabbed that pipe she loves. I pushed in, and her shit was sloppy wet. I went in and out with deep, long strokes. Her ass was moaning so loud, that she was out doing the vent. I picked up the pace and we finished together. I took one of the washcloths, soaped it up, and cleaned her up before I cleaned myself up. I passed her the mouthwash and let her rinse her mouth.

I looked at her through the mirror. I wrapped my arm around her waist and planted small kisses on the back of her neck. "I'm still hungry, baby. When are you going to feed me?" I asked her. She turned in my arms and kissed me on the lips.

"I told you that I gotta feed my baby first." She smiled and walked out the door, leaving me wanting her again. I stayed in the bathroom for a minute to calm down. When I walked out, I bumped into Jason.

"Damn nigga! What happened to you?" I asked him. Jason's mouth was leaking with blood.

"I told you that I was going to deal with the consequences." He said and walked into the bathroom. I walked into the kitchen shaking my head. The children were sitting at the table eating dinner with the women. The men were standing around the kitchen island talking and eating. I fixed my plate and joined in the conversation.

JOEL

～⚬～

      *J*ason had me all the way fucked up. How he gave someone else credit for my work? It wasn't the best, but shit it was mine. The Stand punk ass family members didn't have anything on me. I could have dealt with them all within a week. As soon as his ass told me what he did, I couldn't stop myself if I wanted to. It was a natural reaction. I was sitting at the table listening to the children talk, and Ma-Ma tell Lily that they had to start decorating the nursery.

    Ma-Ma was still mad at me, but she understood why I did what I did. I never wanted to inflict pain on her. Jordan been had that coming. She was lucky that it was me, instead of my brothers or Jason. They ass would have went all the way with it. Jason came walking in, with his lip swollen. I smirked at myself and went over to where the other men were.

    "Ma is it ok if we go back home and show Daddy around." Madison asked.

    "We'll see, Lovie. If your Daddy don't have anything planned, you can ask him." I responded.

    "He doesn't have anything to do. I checked before asking you." Madison said with a smile. I shook my head at her. She was truly spoiled. If Jason did have something to do, he would have canceled it for his children. It was the same way with Poppa. If I needed anything or wanted to see him, he made it happen. Poppa stepped out of many meetings to talk to me when I had a difficult day or when I wanted to hear his voice before I went to sleep. I told myself that, that's what I want for my children.

My phone beeped. I pulled it out and saw that I received a message from the operator. I excused myself and walked out of the backdoor. I dialed nine-two-two and waited for my instructions or my target info. I took hits every now and then to keep my skills on point. And the way that I had been feeling for the past days, made me crave it.

"Target name is Frederick O'Dell and his immediate family. Cleveland, Ohio. One million dollars. An extra five hundred thousand if you remove his heart and send it to Carter Inc. Please press or say one if you accept. Press or say two if you decline."

"I accept." I said and hung up the phone. I went back into the house and placed my phone in my back pocket. Kymel looked over at me and I nodded my head. I went to the table and kissed the children goodbye. I asked Ma-Ma to take care of them and make sure that they do their homework. After today, I was sure that Jason was going to teach them some of his tricks.

I walked over to the table where the men were. "Hey, I got called in. Are you guys going to stay here with the children." I asked Mel and Mani.

"Yeah, but I am not sleeping over. I got somewhere I need to be later tonight. You do know that their father is standing right here." Mani said, pointing at a glaring Jason.

"Right, well I'll see y'all later." I said and turned and walked towards the front door. Jason came behind me and called out my name. I turned to see what he wanted.

"You back working now." He asked me.

"It is really none of your business." I told him and walked out the door. I knew I shouldn't have went to that lunch with him. I heard the door close behind me and prepared for the argument I knew that we were about to have. Before he could touch me, I turned and leaned on my car, facing him.

"You don't think that you should be home with the children and leaving that shit alone." He came straight out and told me.

"If I did leave this shit alone, you and your brothers wouldn't be here." I told him.

"I had that covered. Why don't you call yo people back and tell them that they can give the job to your brothers. We can spend more time with the children together." He demanded.

"Jason, get the fuck out of my face with that. I am going to do this job and there is nothing that you can do about it. You go back in there and spend some time with our children. You the one that missed a lot." I said.

His nose started flaring in and out, like a raging bull. I didn't give a fuck. He had to know that he didn't control nothing over here. "That wasn't my fault." He whispered stepping into my personal space.

"Not your fault." I mocked. "Who fault is it, huh? Jordan. That bitch Mya. Tell me." I began to get angry.

"You already know the answer to that. I'm not about to sit here and go over that shit with you, like you weren't there." He said stepping closer.

"Yeah, I was there. And what I saw, was a weak ass man being controlled by the muthafuckers around him. You are the blame for all this shit Jason. You. You let Jordan do that shit to you when you knew that I wasn't wrong. You underestimated that bitch Mya and she got close enough to get to Pops. It was you! Stop looking to fault other people for your fuck ups. I did it before, but I will not make the same mistake again." I told him and turned this time. I wasn't for his shit tonight. He was the reason why I needed to get away.

"I could see that you need to get a lot more shit off your chest. I'll let you go this time, but don't make this shit a habit. When you get back, be expecting some changes to be made." He said and walked off like he told me something. I didn't bother stopping him. I jumped in my car and headed home. I had to grab some weapons that I was going to use for this job.

I didn't want to come back to this. I always wanted that happily ever after, in a strange way. I had to be a fool to think that I wasn't going to come back. I knew we had enemies out there. Shit, all over. That was one of the main reasons why we didn't show our faces. We didn't want to be hanging out with family, and someone recognize us, then try to kill us and the people we love. That was one of the many ways that our tech was able to track these assholes and their family down. They were all on social media, living receipts of where they been.

I pressed the Bluetooth on my phone and called our tech to get some more background information on my target. "Why are you calling this line?" Tyja asked.

"Because I need some information on Frederick O'Dell and his relatives." I responded. The line went quiet, before I heard her typing on her keyboard. "Don't let Jason drive you to be fucked up like him." She said.

"We both can agree, when I say that I am past that point." I told her.

"Are you sure you want to do this? I mean, the Stand was necessary. They were going to kill your children's father and their uncles. You don't have to justify nothing by doing this job." Tyja told me softly.

She was always the one to pull me off the cliff. I met Tyjaree (Tyja) while we were in high school. She was funny and always had a group of people around her. I, on the other hand, was quiet and didn't care to have friends. I drowned myself in my books, so that I could get the hell out of school. We were in gym and I was looking at some interest tools that I could use for a project that I was working on. A basketball was thrown my way. I picked it up and rolled it over to the boys that were playing with it. I picked my book up and continued doing what I was doing, when the ball came towards me again. I looked over at the boys and Quincy Stevens was smiling at me. I ignored him and the ball. I continued doing what I was doing.

"So, you gon' act like you don't see that ball." Quincy spoke.

NEICY P.

"Yep, just like you acted like you don't see that I don't want to be bothered." I said to him without picking my head up.

"You know what they say about the quiet ones," He responded. The whole gym started laughing, which was something I absolutely hated. I looked up at him with unsettling eyes. His dumb ass didn't get the look. His friend Terry, picked up another ball and threw it towards me. I didn't duck or move. I was hoping that he hit me with it. I wanted to have a reason to beat the shit out of his clique. I knew what I was able to do. I tried my hardest to stay out of trouble because of it. But like my Poppa said, it will only take you to beat that ass once, for the rest to get the point. I was ready for that "once."

The ball hit the wall above my head. "Oh, so you not scared of balls. That's good to know." Terry laughed out with the rest of the boys.

"I heard that you like balls, too. That's why you be in Quincy ass." Tyja told him. The laughing stopped and was replaced with oohs.

"Nobody was talking to you Tyja. Mind yo fucking business." Tyree told her.

"Like she was minding hers. Y'all always dishing out shit but can't take it. Leave that girl alone. She doesn't bother nobody." Tyja yelled at him.

Quincy stepped up to her. "You all big and bad when it comes to helping other people. But where yo fight be when Vantrell be fucking you up." He told her.

I saw what that did to her. If she didn't try to stand up for me, everyone wouldn't have found out her secret. By the gasps around the gym, no one knew but Quincy. "Maybe I'll tell him how you were acting today."

Tyja looked at Quincy uncertainly. She wanted to help me, but she didn't want to get her ass whipped. Tyja smiled and said fuck it. She pulled her fist back and punched Quincy dead in the eye. He stumbled back, holding his face.

"You bitch!" He yelled and charged at her.

Tyja stood with her chin up, bracing herself for impact. She didn't have to worry about it coming. I came from her right and kicked Quincy in the side. He went flying. He went unconscious when his head hit the floor. I stood and waited for his other friends to jump in for him. They scary asses watched like the rest of them. Nobody wanted to be the one to get beat up by the quiet girl. Everyone, except Quincy and Vantrell. I found him and cracked all his ribs *and broke both legs. He was on the football team with a promising future. Not no more. He was going to wish that he never put a hand on Tyjaree.*

"Hey, Joel. Did you hear me?" Tyja came through the speaker. I shook my head and came back to the present.

"Yeah, I'm here. Send me the information, Tyja. I need the floor plans and a number of all the guards that work for them." I told her and hung up. I reached our home and went straight to the basement. I pressed in the code and the wall opened. I walked in and went straight for the knives. We had a lot of guns on the wall, but knives were my specialty. I had three hunting knives, Seax, Bowie knives and one of my favorites, Kukri. I grabbed one of those, with a couple of neck knives and throwing knives. I planned on making it messy. My phone beeped, letting me know that messages were coming through. I pulled it out and saw that Tyja had sent me everything I needed to know about the O'Dells. I changed clothes and called our jet. "Up in thirty." I told the pilot and hung up. I pulled my hair out of its ponytail and sat in the chair, that was in the middle of the room.

I closed my eyes and thought of nothing. Everything that mattered to me, was pushed to the back of my mind. My children. My brothers. My Poppa. Everyone. Including Jason and his family. I took a deep breath in and let it out slowly. I let the darkness ease in. The information that I got from Tyja consumed my mind. I planned out how I was going to kill each one of them. My hand started twitching and my neck needed that familiar crack. I popped it and opened my eyes slowly.

Gage

I sat in the tree that was on the property of the O'Dells. I looked in the window of their house and saw that they were having Sunday dinner. The father was at the head of the table with his four sons and two daughters. Their husbands were there, along with eight of their personal guards. I hated when they made it easy for me. I jumped out of the tree and scrolled over the other four dead guards. I hit their dogs with acid shots. I walked in the front door using the security bracelet that the O'Dells make their guards wear to get in the house.

I walked through the house, looking at pictures and other shit that they had displayed on the walls of their home. I stood by the door and waited for the right time to enter. "How many women did you guys get from the ship?" A deep voice spoke.

"We got forty from the ship last night. They were all young and ripe, too." Another said.

"You should go ahead and let us break them in, Fred. That way, they won't squirm when the customers get them."

"No, we get more for virgins. You can teach them how to suck though." One of the women said and at that point it was my time to make my appearance. I walked in, twirling one of my throwing knives.

"Suh, yuh wa dem to suffa as yuh did." I said to the crowd. The guards quickly stood up and pulled their weapons.

"Who the fuck is you?" The father asked, while sitting back in his chair. Freddrick O'Dell was a sloppy looking muthafucker. He was the type to have to lift his head up to the sky and breathe. The children didn't take after him. They were slim and fit. I leaned against the wall with eight guns pointed at me. Two of the guards went and stood next to him while the others circled the rest of the family.

I ignored his question and waited for the woman to answer my question. The oldest son pulled his gun out and sat it on the table. Frank O'Dell. He was the overachiever. The one that always went the extra two miles to please his father. The shit was pathetic. The other sons followed his lead and did whatever he asked. He made an example out of his two daughters. They were sold to their father's highest bidders when they were younger. When they got older, the two moved back with their father and started running this fucked up business with them.

One of the guards moved closer to me, with his gun still pointed at me. "Who are you, bitch?" He asked.

"Dat a nuh di right question to ask. Yuh question should be, why mi here." I said to them. Freddrick frowned up at me with confusion. He looked over to his sons and shook his head.

"What the fuck did she just say?" He asked them.

"I don't know, Dad." The oldest stood with his gun in his hand. I didn't bother repeating myself. One of their guards knew exactly what I said. He was from my country. I smiled at him, knowing that he already knew who I was but didn't want to believe it. He looked down at his gun and knew that it wouldn't stop me. With his head down, he translated for them.

"She said that we asked the wrong question. Why she is here, is what we really need to know." He whispered and took a step back. Freddrick looked over at him and grunted.

"Ok, why are you here." He asked smugly.

This time I spoke in perfect English. I didn't want the guard to repeat anything I said. I was ready to see blood. His subtitles were going to slow me down.

"Many have a problem with your...business. You take young girls and boys from their family to sell them to the highest bidder. Some of you men and sons had raped a few of them. They voted, and you have been judged." I told him. Freddrick looked around again and started laughing. The men and the women began to laugh with him. All but the one guard that was standing on the wall, saying a silent prayer.

"Are you serious? They sent you to teach me a lesson." He laughed out. He pushed back his seat and patted his knee. "Why don't you come and punish me then little girl. Come show me how bad of a man I have been." He asked me.

I stopped twirling my knife and glared over at him with a disturbing smile. "If that is what you want." I replied and threw my knife in the neck of the guard that was standing next to him. He started shooting and shot two guards in the chest. I pulled out another knife and grabbed the arm of the guard that was standing next to me and stabbed him in his armpit twice. I spun behind him and stabbed him in the back of his throat. I threw another knife in the arm of the guard to my left, while the other one started shooting. I hit the husband of one of the daughters on top of his head. I kicked his seat

NEICY P.

from under him. He tried to swing on me but was dizzy from the hit. I spun him around and used him as a shield for the bullets that were coming my way. I picked up the plate that he was eating out of and threw it like a Frisbee to the other husband that was sitting next to the youngest daughter. He fell out of his chair, from the impact. By that time, the guard that was shooting was nervously trying to reload his weapon.

The guard that I threw the knife at pulled the knife out of his arm and came charging at me with it. I grabbed his arm, snapped it, which caused the knife to go up into the air. I snapped his neck, leaned on the table and kicked the fallen knife into the shooter's head. Freddrick's main guard grabbed me from behind. I slammed my head back and heard the crunch of his nose. He dropped me and tried reaching for me with one hand, while the other was trying to stop the blood from leaking out of his nose. I dodged his arms and was now kneeling behind him. I pulled out a booth knife and sliced through his Achilles. When he fell forward, I made sure that my favorite blade was there to pierce through his heart.

I got up and now the sons were out their seat with their guns. The girls were now standing next to the other guard who didn't bother fighting back. He knew that no one was going to make it out of here alive. I kicked my last kill over and pulled the blade out of his chest. I didn't know why the sons didn't fire their weapons. It was always a male thing with wanting to gloat about who they kill. Even after seeing what I was capable of, they still thought that they had a chance.

I looked over to the shivering guard and shook my head. "Yuh kno dat dis shit frowned pon inna yuh fambly. But yuh ova har, working fi dem. Supporting dis shit like demy uh fada neva send mi fi get Karma." I told him. His eyes opened wider now that he knew who he was up against. He closed his eyes and bowed his head.

"What the fuck is going on here? Benton, what is she saying? Did you set us up muthafucker?" The Freddrick yelled at him. His oldest son didn't wait for him to answer. He raised his gun up, which singled the girls to move away from Benton. When they were in the clear. He shot him three times in the head and then turned his gun to me.

"Now. I am going to ask you one more time. Who the fuck is you?" He asked with a little growl at the end.

I looked at everyone in the room, before my eyes rested on Freddrick. "I am Gage." I told them in a whisper. All their eyes widened at my declaration. The husband of the youngest daughter finally stood with blood rolling down his face. Whatever he was trying to say was lost to the darkness and gunfire. One by one, I sliced them open. Their screams began to drown out the shooting, leaving only one man breathing. The lights came back on and Freddrick was still sitting in his seat with that dick look.

He kept his eyes on me as I stalked over to him. I straddled his lap and smirked at his bewildered look. "I am Gage, Freddrick. Your executioner." I told him and with a quick movement my blade was opening his throat. I sat as he tried to reach for his neck. I took each hand and cut it off. He bucked, and I stood, as he fell to the floor. I watched as he struggled with the death that was sure to win. He gurgled and tried to talk to me. I looked through him like I was doing everything else. I broke eye contact with Frederick and looked around the room. I saw all the dead bodies spread around. I took a deep breath in and sighed. This was something that I thought I could give up. I was doing just fine, 'til I bumped into Jason at the grocery store. I was in my happy place. I fucked up and let him in.

Everyone was fine, now. My brothers and father accepted him into our family. Jordan apologized to his family, and he was building a relationship back with his brothers. My children see Jason as some type of long-lost hero, that I painted him out to be. I should be ok right. But I wasn't. I was pissed.

I sacrificed a lot to be with him. I opened up just like he did and trusted him to do right by me. And at the first sight of trouble, he turned on me and blamed everybody else for his shit. Not once did anybody think to apologize to me. *Hey Joel, sorry that I wasn't there when you gave birth to our children. Or, Joel I'm sorry that you had to raise our kids on your own, while I was wilding out and fucking random bitches.* I beat Jordan's ass, true. But, I was still waiting on an apology from him. No, I didn't deserve that, though.

And come to think of it, it was a lot more shit that was bothering me when I thought about it. I was the one to bottle shit up and took it as it was. Even when my mother died unexpectedly, I sat at her funeral and shed no tears. Poppa told me that it was ok for me to cry for losing her. But I didn't want to cry. Death was the norm for me. I caused pain and death for many. Me and my mother's relationship was great. I just didn't understand her and my father's relationship. After she had me, she didn't date or anything. She stayed singled hoping that my Poppa would stop with his shit, so that they could be together. She waited for my Poppa just like my stupid ass was waiting on Jason.

I went along with the bullshit. Never had I ever asked for an explanation on shit. The only thing that I got was, *when you come back, things were going to change.* Yeah, muthafucker. You are right about that. Some things were going to change.

I went to walk away and saw that I was on top of Frederick. His chest had several puncture wounds. I had blood everywhere. To tell you the truth, I didn't recognize Frderick no more. His face had wounds in them as well. I stood up with my blade ready for my next kill. I gathered all my knives and walked out the front door. My Parrain walked over to me and stared. Usually when I was done with a hit, I came down from my high as soon as I walked out of the building. That time, he saw something in me that he had never seen before. I didn't bother acknowledging his look. I walked past him, while stripping out of my clothes.

"Go back home, Punisher. This job is done."

JASON

Joel had been missing for a couple of weeks now. No one had heard from her. The kids were asking about her. Kymani and Kymel told them that she was on an important job. They understood that and went ahead with the training and their assignments. I didn't know how I felt about being that honest with them. I was helping Mason with some of his math, well watched him solve his math problems, when my phone started ringing. I was hoping that it was Joel calling to check on the children. I pulled it out and saw that it was a number that I didn't recognize.

I swiped to answer. "Who this?"

"Jason, my boy. You are a hard person to get in touch with. How are you?" Leon Williams asked.

I let out a frustrated breath. I didn't want to be bothered with this shit today or never. Sierra had been calling and texting, still. I ignored her and continued spending time with my children. I guess she got tired of being ignored and called her father. That's what spoiled bitches do.

"What is it that you want, Leon? I'm busy." I told him flat out and bored with the conversation already.

"Well I have a proposition for you and your family? I would like to meet up today, with you and your brothers. Is eight good?" He asked.

"No, eight is not good. Matter of fact, never is good. We don't need your business." I said ready to hang up.

"I didn't think that the Davis crew would turn down a business deal without hearing it out." He continued. I thought about it a little more before answering him. I knew that I didn't want to deal with them anymore. The meeting couldn't hurt.

"Ten. We could meet at ten. I'll text you the address." I told him and hung up. I wanted to put my children to sleep at eight. I got up and walked out of the room, to look for Jordan to let him know about this meeting with Leon. He had been spending a lot of time with JoJo before the other baby got here.

They were outside playing football with JJ and my cousins. Ma and Auntie Glen were sitting down with Madison watching them. I ran out and intercepted the football right out of Tank's hand. The fool pushed me and called it a lucky catch.

"Not luck, T. It's the skills." I told him and started laughing.

"Yeah right. Yo ass can't fuck with me in football. You better stick to what you know, nigga." He told me and snatched the ball out of my hand. I walked over to Jo and signaled all the men to bring it in.

"Hey JoJo, come get some of your Nana's sweet tea baby. I made it just how you like it." Ma said.

"Yeah, like syrup." JJ mumbled.

"I heard that JJ. Don't make me come over there." Ma told him.

Jo walked over to the table while we talked. "I just got off the phone with Leon Williams. He wants to meet up with us at ten." I told them.

"For fucking what. Marquel already supply us with the weapons that we need. What else is he offering?" Jo asked. Everyone nodded their head in agreement.

"I don't know, man. I think it has something to do with me blowing off his daughter." I responded and looked up at Jo. "Look Jo, I don't know what else they have planned. I told them that I was going to send them the address to where I want them to meet us. If they are planning something, they are going to try and get their early to set up. Two hours, tops. I figure we can send some men over there before them."

"Where are we meeting them?" JJ asked.

"The Center." I told them. We all haven't been to the Center since Pops died. That was the one place that I knew that we could meet them up at and have the upper hand. It was a big open space, away from people. Jo nodded his head and started barking orders.

"Aight. Send six of our best shooters out there. Tank, I want you out there, too. Tristian, I want you to find out where they are staying. Send men out there and have them followed. I want to know every move they make and how many are traveling with him." Kymel and Kymani stepped in while Jo was talking.

"We don't mind tagging along. We can sit up in the meeting with y'all. It would shake things up when they see that you have new people with you. Especially if they had been studying the Davis crew." Kymel spoke.

"I agree. We could leave here around eight-thirty." I told them. I called up Dex to get me the information I needed. He answered on the second ring.

"What's up J?"

"I need information on Leon Williams. Any info on his business transactions and who he had done it with. I also need to know what his sons been doing. I don't know the name of his other son. He is not in this business. Alan and Brandon Williams are over some businesses up north. Find out what they do and how they do it. I need this information at six." I told him.

"Cool, I get it to you at five." He said and hung up. Dex and Tristan been hanging out a lot. They been building some type of security system for the family to use. We all were wearing watches that were programmed by Dex and Tristan. We were able to make calls and send out an alert when something was wrong.

After that, we all separated and went on with our day. Ma cooked with the women as the men hung out and watched the game. We all ate dinner. After that, Kymel took out some cards so that we can play some spades. Mel and Mani were busting ass and taking names. JJ thought that they were cheating. He was always a sore loser.

I went upstairs to check on the quiet children. I got to the room and heard them whispering. "Mace, you better put that away before Daddy catch you." Madison told him.

"If you would be quiet, no one will catch me." Mason replied. I could hear him grunting through the door.

"Daddy won't find you because of my whispering. He will find you because he is going to leave our uncles downstairs to come check on us. He is probably at the door right now." Madison said. I smiled and opened the door with Madison playing with her dolls and Mason playing with his game. I knew his little ass was up in here playing with them weapons. "Hi Daddy. You are about to go?" He asked without looking up at me.

I could see the smile on Madison's face. She knew I was standing at the door. When she made that promise to her mother, she planned on keeping it. Even if she had to rat out her brother to do it. I walked over to him with my hand out.

"Give it to me, Mason." I told him in my stern voice. He dropped his head and reached under the pillow that he was sitting on. He pulled out a blade and placed it in my hand. "How many times did your mother ask you to not play with weapons in the house?" I asked him.

"A lot." He mumbled. "I'm sorry, Dad." He said. It didn't sound like he was trying to bullshit me. I wanted to make sure that he understood what would happen the next time.

"I understand that you are sorry. But if I catch you doing this again, we are going to have some problems. You understand that." I said. He stood up and looked at me.

"Yes, sir." he answered.

"Good. It's bedtime. Let's go."

Madison began to put her dolls away. Mason walked to his bed and jumped in. I asked if he wanted to share a room with JoJo. He told me that it was best if he stayed close to his sister. I walked over to Madison's bed first and kissed her on the cheek.

"Good night, Pretty Girl. I'll see you in the morning."

"Ok, Daddy. Be safe tonight. Love you." She said to me.

"I love you too. Get some rest." I told her and walked over to Mason's bed. I leaned over and kissed him on the forehead. "Good night, Lil Man. Get some rest. We will talk more about these weapons on tomorrow." I told him.

He nodded his understanding. "Ok, Dad. Good night. Love you." He told me.

"I love you, too." I told him and walked out of their room. I walked downstairs and saw that the guys were ready as well. Jo was walking down the stairs after me.

"Y'all ready." He asked.

"Yeah, let's get this over with." I told him. We all jumped in the SUVs and drove to the Center. Kymel and Kymani was riding with me. Kymani was in the back on the phone, while we were listening to music.

"Damn it!" We heard Kymani yelled.

"After this is over, we gotta get Joel." He said while looking at his phone.

I stopped the car in the middle of the street and put it in park. I wished a muthafucker would blow their horn at me too.

"Is she alright?" I turned and asked him.

He shook his head before answering, "I don't know, man. She had been taking jobs back to back. Our pilot dropped her off at home after the first hit. After that, she had been taking the jet on her own. She also interrupted the operator and started receiving calls directly. Our tech tried to track the GPS on the jet, but Joel removed it, along with the one that was on her phone. What's bothering me the most are the pictures of her work. This shit looks brutal, man." He said, handing over the phone.

I grabbed it and looked at the pictures. It looked like she was in pure rage with each one of those jobs. There was blood everywhere. Body parts were missing from the bodies. The shit looked horrible.

"We can call this meeting off. I gotta get to her." I said. I was about to make a U-turn. Kymel stopped me.

NEICY P.

"Let's take care of this first. Our tech got to find where she is at first. It doesn't make sense to be sitting around waiting." I was seriously debating on going to this meeting. My phone rung through the Bluetooth of the car. I knew that Jo was wondering why we stopped.

"Yeah," I answered.

"Yo, everything good." Jo asked.

"Man, I don't know. We just received some news about Joel." I told him.

"Hey J, we can handle this. Go and check on your woman." He said and that surprised me. Usually, he was all about getting the job done. He was about family now and that would have made Pops proud.

"No, we are going to deal with this first. We are on the way." Mani said from the backseat.

"You sure." Jo asked. He was really talking to me. I looked over at her brothers and they both were staring at me with blank expressions. I shook my head and put the car in drive. "Yeah, I'm sure. We are on our way." I told him and hung up. I knew that she could handle herself. I just needed her to be alright mentally.

We got to the Center and parked behind Jo. They walked over to the car and waited for us to get out. "Hey, my sister is alright. Don't let that shit interfere with this shit here." Kymani said and got out with his brother. I took a deep breath and opened the door. Jo and JJ were right there.

"You alright, bruh." JJ asked. Jo must have told him what was going on.

"Yeah, I'm good. Did you get word on where they at?" I asked, changing the subject.

"Zaire told us that they were going to be here in ten minutes. Everything is already set up inside." Jo replied. "Everybody else get in position!" He yelled. We walked into the Center and saw the big table sitting in the middle, surrounded by chairs. Jo took the seat in the middle. JJ and I flanked him, while Kymel and Kymani stood behind us. Them niggas placed them hoods on their heads and let their dreads down. It was an intimidation tactic that always worked for them.

THE WAY TO A KILLER'S HEART 2

We all heard them pulling up outside. Two of our guards opened the doors and directed them to pull in the warehouse. They were riding deep with two SUVs and a cold ass black Excursion. The men started getting out and lined up against the Excursion that was in the middle. One of the guards opened the door and Sierra's brother, Alan stepped out first. After him, was Leon and his other son, Brandon. Leon led the group over to the table. They took their seats on the other side of the table with six of their men standing behind them. The others stayed with the vehicles. He didn't send none of his men outside, which let me know that he already had some out there already.

Brandon had his eyes on me, while Alan was mugging JJ. Leon directed his attention to Jo but couldn't stop looking over our shoulders at Kymel and Kymani. Jo shook his head and smirked. "I don't think you called us to meet up, so that we can have a staring contest. You said that you have a business proposition for us. Let's hear it."

"Straight to business, I like that. Jason was telling my daughter that you guys were looking for more connections out in the west. We pretty much run the west and some states in the north. The Brooks are losing customers and their distributors out there. Their products are weak. We heard that you all got that Grade A shit. My boys could easily run the Brooks out and any other suppliers, if you are willing to set up camp out in the west. I'm pretty sure that Jason wouldn't mind doing this. I heard that him and Sierra was getting close." Leon smiled at me.

See. Bullshit. There was no way that I was leaving my children to move out west with that bitch. I knew that she had something to do with this shit. Leon was trying to capitalize on it, by bringing her name up. I didn't know what she told him, but I needed to set him straight on a few things. Jo placed his elbows on the table and leaned forward. He also knew that this was some bullshit.

"Your offer ain't tempting at all, man. First, I know that my brother didn't tell yo daughter shit about what we are looking for. He is not the pillow talking type. Second, we are not looking to expand shit. We are good where we at and if we did want to take over the West, we wouldn't need your help to do that. The DW's make sure we get what we need at a reasonable price. I heard that they are about to take over the west." Jo said.

"They already got the whole north, which your...sons were supposed to have." JJ spoke out. "Another lie you told."

"That is true. We just talked to Marquel about this." I jumped in. Jo nodded his head and looked over at a Leon.

"Yeah. I remember that. So, you see Leon, you are not needed. At all. Thanks for wasting my time." Jo said to them. They sat there like Jo didn't just dismiss them. Leon leaned forward this time with a smirk on his face.

"Well, I was hoping that we could do this the easy way." He said and looked over at his sons that were now smiling with him as well. "We heard what happened to the Stand. We also heard that the Davis crew was in attendance. How is it that you all walked out alive?" He said to us.

Jo's expression didn't change. He stared at Leon and waited to see if that was all he got. When Leon didn't continue, Jo started laughing. "You mean that was what you came up with. You thought that you could blackmail us into working with you by spreading lies." He asked with amusement. The smirk dropped from Leon's face. He really thought that he had us. That was another reason why you would never catch us working with them. They were some conniving muthafuckers.

Leon glared at Jo like he wanted to jump across the table. "You laugh now but it won't be so funny when they come for your family." He looked over at me. "And yours. I heard about the little family you got. You were fucking with that bitch and my daughter. You should be lucky that I came and tried to reason with you and your family. Other niggas that fucked over her, got hot ones in them for doing less." He said to me. I eased up a little to make sure I heard what this nigga said.

"You right Pops, but you gotta give it to this nigga, though. That bitch is bad. Little Miss Joel Smith from New Orleans and a graduate from LSU. She has a few houses in a couple of states." Brandon said, staring at me. "Oh, I looked her up. I was thinking that I could go and

THE WAY TO A KILLER'S HEART 2

pay her a visit after this. I don't know why an independent woman like that would settle for a nigga like you. And the kids. Shit, they have to settle for a nigga that only come around them sometimes. Nah, Ima fixed that. I'll make sure that they get-"

POW!

Guns went off around the building. We didn't bother moving, because all our people had accurate aim. Jo and JJ already had their guns out. Shadow was lurking over me trying to get to an already dead Brandon. The nigga was going too fucking far. I placed my gun on the table and waited 'til our crew got rid of Leon's men.

Leon was staring at his son's brain all over his suit. Alan looked pissed off but at the end of the day, I didn't give a fuck. You never threatened a man's family in their face and think that you were going to walk out here alive. After the smoke cleared and all their men were dead. I looked over to Leon.

"Is there anything that any of you niggas want to add about my woman or children?" I asked. "Nothing. Are you sure? Alan. Something to say." When they both sat there mugging me, I continued. "That's what the fuck I thought." I said and got up. I had to go and take care of more important shit than this. Alan reached for his gun and Jo shot him. JJ said the hell with it and shot Leon.

Shadow walked over to Brandon and pulled his head back. He pulled out a knife and cut Brandon's tongue out, then put it in his pocket. "He won't be able to talk in hell." He said and walked off, like what he just did was normal. We all walked out and met up with Tank and the other shooters. Tank was shaking his head smiling. "He said something about Joel, huh." He asked.

"And Mason and Madison." JJ spat out.

"Oh, yeah. He lucky you didn't take him to the theater." Tank replied.

"I didn't have time to play with that punk ass nigga." I looked over at Shadow and Reap. "Did you hear anything?" I asked them. They had their heads up in the air like they were enjoying a good dream. Shadow stumbled back and caught himself on the wall. We all were looking at them.

"Yo bruh, you alright." Jo asked them.

"She just made another kill." Kymani mumbled.

"How you know that?' I asked.

"We could feel it. Every time she makes a kill, we can feel that shit." Kymel whispered.

"What it feels like?" Tank asked.

"it's the best euphoric feeling ever. It's like busting a nut." Kymani said while leaning against the wall.

JJ looked over at me and Jo. "Why our connection ain't that deep? Y'all fucking up big time."

"Shut yo simple ass up." I told him. This nigga looked big mad, for real. I turned my attention back to Kymel. He pulled his phone out and checked his message. Whatever he saw had his mouth dropped open. He showed it to Kymani and his expression was the same.

"We gotta get to the house. Our father is waiting there." Kymani said and walked off.

"Yo, is she alright. What did you see?" I asked, following behind them.

"She is not hurt. We just gotta set up a plan to see her. If we go at her wrong, she might do something to us." Kymel said. We jumped in the car and headed home. Once we got there, everybody jumped out and went into the house. Ma and T Glen was sitting on the couch with Joel's father and another man that I haven't seen before. I nodded to them and went upstairs to check on my children. I walked into their room and kissed them both, before walking out again.

When I got back downstairs, Kymel was showing his father the pictures on his phone. "Wen did dis start?" Callum asked.

"She left a couple weeks ago for a job. We haven't seen her since." Kymani told him.

Callum was swiping through the photos and got to the last one. He looked up at his sons and the other man and shook his head. "Get di tech here." He said.

"She is already on her way." Kymel answered.

"I can also call my tech over. Tristan is also good with computers and shit." I told them.

"Gud get dem all here. Wi need fi find har." Callum said. I pulled out my phone and texted Dex. Tristan was already setting up in the office. Ma and T Glenda went to the kitchen, while the men went into the big office and waited for the other techs to arrive. Tristan pulled up the pictures from Kymel's phone and displayed them on the big screen. Everyone was amazed at what they were seeing. Nobody would have thought that a woman like Joel, could do something like that.

"Why the bodies look drained?" Jo asked.

"Because they are. It was something we do when we were over the edge. She drained their blood, to bathe in it." Kymani said.

"Hold up. What did you say?" JJ asked. Everybody had the same expression on their faces. The shit was unreal. I never caught myself wanting to bathe in muthafuckers' blood. That was that new crazy.

"It's one of our rituals. Some men would send the sons out into the jungle to hunt for their own food. When they come back with the meat of their prey, they also came back with the blood all over them. The blood represents the kill." The other man spoke.

"Who are you?" I asked.

He smirked and shook his head. "I am the Punisher." He said and turned back to the screen. The fucking Punisher. This shit was getting crazier by the minute. JJ was tapping Jo on the shoulder in pure shock.

"Yo, did that nigga say he was the Punisher." He asked.

Jo nodded his head. We were all speechless. "He is Joel's Parrain and her teacher." Kymani said.

Well, that explains everything. The Punisher was known for his techniques all around the world. Some of the training that we did in the Navy came from him. The door opened and in walked Dex with his many computers.

"Where am I setting up at?" He asked. I pointed over to Tristan and Dex got right to work. We were going to do all the introductions later. Right now, we had to find Joel.

"What do we have to go on?" Dex asked when he got caught up to speed.

"Some pictures that were sent to her brother's phone from the clients." Tristan told him, still punching on his keys. Dex pulled up the map of the United States and red dots started to appear. "These are all of the places she has been in the weeks she was missing." He said. I counted eighteen dots. Joel been real busy. "I need to know the IP address on the jet. I can find her like that." Tristan asked.

"I can give you that." A woman's voice spoke by the door. We all turned back and saw that it was Tyja. JJ jumped up and was about to address her. She held up her hand and stopped him. "Now is not the right time. We can talk after I find my sister." She told him and opened her computer. She started punching keys with the other Tecs. Tyja's phone started beeping and she pulled the message up on the screen. The last job that Joel did was displayed on the screen.

"Why does these kills look so personal? She never did this?" Kymani whispered. Callum walked up to the screen silently and looked at it. He dropped his head and let out a sigh.

"I think I know what this is about." He said and turned around to face us. The screen started ringing and we all looked back at the screen.

"I found her." Tyja said. "You better hurry. She only stays in one spot for hours, if that. The other jet is fueled up and ready for take-off." She said and typed at the same time. Everyone's phone started beeping. I pulled it out and saw the destination.

"I think it would be best if Jason was the only one to come with us." Kymani said. "We will make sure that he comes home safe."

"Aight," Jo said and walked over to me. "Bring your woman home." He said. JJ walked up to me and said the same thing. We dapped it up and I followed behind Joel's family. When we got into the car, Callum looked over at me and started talking.

"She will try to provoke us to fight. Don't let her. She doesn't need us to be hostile. She need understanding." He told me.

"She got that." I said and was ready to be there for her, like she was for me.

SHAN PRESENTS MARCH MAYHEM CONTEST!

Secret Code: SP0300215

Want a chance to win a $10 gift card, be sure to one click this hot new release, find the secret code, and email it to spreadingcontests@gmail.com. NO SCREENSHOTS! Be sure to hold on to your code, and watch out for all of Shan Presents releases between 03/1-03-31 to collect all the codes for your chance to be entered to win one of 5 cash prizes!

JOEL

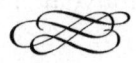

I just finished off another job. Clients have been calling me non-stop now that they see that I was back in business. I flew to one of our safe houses in Indiana. None of us barely used the spot. I was just coming here to clean myself up and then, on to my next job. I knew that my family was probably worried about me. But I wasn't done relieving sixteen years of stress.

I got out my car and headed for the front door. As soon as I placed my hand on the knob, I knew that they were here. I could have easily turned around and pulled out before any of them came out. I wasn't the running type, though. I opened the door and went into the family room. All the men that mattered to me was standing, waiting for my arrival.

"Why yuh here?" I asked in a quiet tone. Kymel stepped forward and spoke first.

"Wah gawn wid yuh sis?" He asked. He looked concerned. They all did.

"Wah yuh mean? Mi working." I told him. He shook his head before responding.

"Nuh like dis." He said. I was getting bored with this shit.

"Why are you here?" I asked again.

"We came here to help you." Kymani stepped in. I looked over at him and glared.

"Why would I need your help? Any of you?" I told him and then rested my eyes on Jason who was leaning against the wall with his eyes on me. I saw Mani shake his head.

"We are not here for that." He said. My smile widened at those words.

"Oh, who is going to stop me?" I asked.

"Don't do this alright. I made a promise that I will bring him back alive, El." Mani told me.

I looked back at him and sneered. "How you make that promise, when you can't promise yourself that you will make it out here alive." Mani closed his eyes and opened them back with love in them.

"It won't work."

"Well if it won't, don't interfere. I have other shit to do." I said and turned around. My father's voice stopped me.

"Is there something you want to say?" He asked me. I stopped with my back still towards them. I had a lot to say, but I rather let my gun or knife talk. I reached for my forty-five and held it in my hand. That didn't stop my father from talking though. "You have the floor Joel. Say what you gotta say, Baby Girl."

I turned and faced the men again. "What is it that you want me to say Poppa?"

"Everything. You are trying to say something through your work and I am sorry that I am not a mind reader. I should have caught onto it the first time you made your first kill. But I didn't think nothing of it. I am listening now Joel. Talk to me. Talk to Poppa." He said with so much emotions. It was rare when I see Poppa in this form. He was always strong and didn't show his feelings. It was the same thing that he taught us to do. I guess, at that moment he was trying to lead by example. I didn't know if I wanted to fall in line, like I always did, or just walk off. Poppa was pleading with me to talk to him with his eyes. I broke eye contact and looked over at the person that I knew was going to give me what I was looking for.

"Tired of being a father yet. Is that the reason you came here? To give my children back to me so that you could be with your bitch." I told Jason. He got up from the wall and was about to walk towards me. Mani stopped him, and Poppa stepped forward again.

"Joel stop this."

"Stop what Poppa? Stop talking to my children's father. Stop trying to figure out if he is in the right state of mind to be around my children. Cause Lord knows he don't exercise self-control." I replied.

"And you do? Do you have control over yourself? Because to us, it looks like you lost it. This shit that you are doing is showing us that you have gone mad." Poppa told me.

"I am not doing this, Poppa, because I done went mad. No. I am doing this because I am tired. I am tired of bottling shit in and taking it as is. I am tired of making excuses for the habits of others just to make sense out of it. My whole life I lived not knowing why things were the way they were. I sucked it up and moved on. Just like you taught me." I yelled and pointed the gun at myself. "Just like she showed me." I said and then tossed it to the ground. "This is not Gage killing, it's Joel. I am doing this. I could stop if I wanted to, but I don't because, I. AM. TIRED! Joel and Gage is one in the same." Poppa took a step towards me and I backed up shaking my head. "No." I told him.

"She waited her whole life for you and you never went back to her." I whispered.

"My relationship with your mother was something that you would not have understood at that age." He told me.

I balled my fist up at that excuse he made and punched the nearest wall. "I was too young. I was able to kill and torture men you assigned me to. I graduated out of high school at the age of fifteen and college when I was eighteen. I'm pretty sure that, if you would have told me that you weren't ready to settle down with my mother, it would have been nothing to decode." I whispered harshly.

Poppa nodded his head in understanding. "It wasn't that I thought you were too dumb to understand, El. Anyone can read about love but don't understand it until you actually went through it. Your mother wanted me to change and that was true. But I knew that if I would have changed, it still wouldn't have kept her safe from my enemies.

People would have found out about us and I would have been spending my time protecting her, instead of enjoying her. Do you know of the pain that I would have suffered, if your mother's death was because of something I did? I would have never forgiven myself and neither would you." He said. "You know of that feeling, yes." He asked.

I didn't want to agree with him, so I shook my head. "I will never be like my mother. I will never settle for an incompetent man who can't control his self. Ain't no love that deep Poppa." I replied instead.

"But you have, Joel. You haven't been with anyone since Jason. You devoted your time to your children and your business. Just like your children, you waited for him to get better to come back to you." Mel spoke.

I let out a sarcastic laugh. "And he still didn't get better. I had to go and save him from all the bullshit that happened before my children. I didn't do that for him. I did it for them. They deserve to see their father. To have them by their side when they want him and not only when they need him." I yelled at Kymel.

They were always around my father. They didn't understand what I was talking about. Poppa made sure I had the best of everything. But what I craved the most was him being there for me more than he was. When I went to his home in Jamaica, I was always left with someone. We had our moments here and there, but that wasn't shit to count on. I didn't want my children to feel this resentment towards Jason. That was another reason why I came up with them stories.

"Dat ow yuh feel precious?" Poppa sounded hurt.

"I don't want to talk about this shit no more. Y'all leave now or you won't be able to when I come back down." I said quickly and turned around.

"Mi sorry dawta. Dat did neva mi intent. Mi get use to raising boys, dat mi neva realize dat me did neglecting yuh still. Mi tink eff mi give yuh wah yuh ask fi an protecting yuh did gud enuff. Mi did wrong an mi sorry." Poppa said.

I heard the hurt and disappointment in his voice. It wasn't something that a daughter ever wanted to see in her father's eyes. I nodded

NEICY P.

my head and walked slowly upstairs before I broke down. Hearing what my father said lifted a huge weight off my shoulders. I thought that he was going to argue with me, but he didn't He understood and didn't come at me with anger, like I hoped he would have done. I was hoping that they all did.

I opened the door to my room. I closed and then locked it. I removed the weapons from my body and fell to the floor. Nothing mattered more to a woman than a father's love. It didn't matter how old we got. If we got validations from them, on anything, nothing else mattered. I laid there for thirty minutes, still soaked in blood. I stood up and went into the bathroom to start my shower. I came back out to gather some clothes, but I saw that the shower was going to wait. Jason was sitting on the bed staring at me. I leaned against the wall and folded my arms.

"You think I'm incompetent, Joel." He asked. I rubbed my hands together to try and get the tingling feeling out.

"Very," I said and walked over to my closet to get me some clothes out of there. When I turned around, Jason was standing in the doorway staring at me still.

"If I was so incompetent, Joel, why leave the children with me? Why not call to check on them?"

"Do you think that my brothers were there to bond with you?" I chuckled. "They were there for them. And as far as me calling to check on the children, I knew that they were ok, just like they knew that I was ok. I would have felt if something was wrong when them, vice versa." I told him and tried to walk out of the closet. "Get the fuck out of my way." I told him.

"Why did you wait for me, Joel?" He whispered.

"I didn't," I said quickly.

"You didn't wait for me to come home to you. Because that's what you are, Joel. You are home. Always have been." He said walking me back into the closet.

"Get the fuck out of here, Jason. I wasn't shit to you. And you proved that the moment-" I went in, but he interrupted me by placing his hands on my face.

"I'm sorry, Joel." He whispered.

I looked up at him with disbelief. I wanted to believe that this was him saying this to me, but I couldn't. This shit couldn't be real, was what I kept telling myself. I placed my hand on his wrist ready to remove them from my face.

"I'm sorry, El. I never meant to hurt you or cause you that type of pain. I'm sorry that I wasn't the man you needed me to be. I'm sorry that I made the wrong choice. You and the children mean more to me than you will ever know. The joy that I feel of having them around is because of you. Their mother. I'm sorry that I wasn't there then, but I am now. Let me be here for you, baby." He whispered and placed his lips on mine.

Alright y'all. I told y'all that I haven't been with a man since Jason. So, when his lips touched mine, my legs almost buckled. His lips caressed mine slowly and gently. He slipped his tongue into my mouth teasingly then pulled it back out. I let out a soft moan that couldn't be held back. He pulled back and grabbed my hand.

"Let's get you cleaned up." He told me and pulled me into the running shower. Once we got into the bathroom, he began to undress me. After all my clothes were discarded, he started taking off his. He led me into the hot shower and bathed me thoroughly. His hands rubbed up and down my body. When it was time to wash my sacred spot, he took his time. The way that he was handling me almost made me explode. After my body was scrubbed and smelled clean, he stepped out the tub to retrieve my towel.

I stepped out and let him pat me dry. He whispered how much he had to make up to me. I didn't interrupt him. I stood there and listened to every word he said and hung onto them. After I was dry, he walked me over to the bed and placed me on it. I tried to grab that delicious piece that was hanging from him like an elephant's trunk. My mouth got watery looking at it. He stepped back and shook his head.

"I need you to lay back, baby." He told me. "This is your night."

I bit on my bottom lip and eased on back. He started to kiss my ankle on my right leg and worked his way up. He bit the inside of my thigh and that shit had me jumping up. He placed his hand flat on my stomach to hold me down.

"Be a good girl for me and be still, baby." He mumbled. I tried to gain some type of control over my body, but I was failing miserably. Without warning, he placed his thick tongue over my button like a warm blanket.

"Fuuck, Jason." I groaned out loud. I hoped that my family left for the night because I was making all types of noises. He licked then sucked, sucked and then licked. He was driving me insane. My leg started shaking and I came all over his face. He didn't let that stop him. He kept sucking on my shit like it was a frozen cup from Granny's out the seventh ward.

I was twisting and turning ready for him to slide his eleven-inch pole inside of me. He finally came up for air and kissed me on my lips. My vitamin c was all over his face. I tasted myself on his lip and got turned on all over again. He lifted my legs up and I wrapped my arms around his neck. He lifted me up and pushed me further up in the bed. I felt his pole slide up and down against my button.

"My peach is still juicy and sweet. I love the way you taste El. Your shit is addictive." He said to me while kissing me tenderly on my neck.

"Come on, Jason and fuck me." I demanded. He picked his head up and shook his head.

"You don't need to get fucked, El. You need these nice and deep strokes. That's what you need." He replied and slid into me. Perfect fucking fit. We both moaned out each other's name. I started rotating my hips, wanting to feel him stretch me more. He pulled out to the tip and eased back in. "Shit, baby. You kept this pussy tight for me." He muttered. I tried to speed up his movements, but he kept it nice and slow. He sat up and took my nipple into his mouth.

"Yaaass, J. Just like that. Make me come again on this dick." I whimpered out.

He let my nipple go and looked down at me. "You are mine, El. I love you." He told me.

Before I could respond, I felt that tense feeling, letting me know that I was on the verge of falling over. His movements didn't increase.

THE WAY TO A KILLER'S HEART 2

He kept going, while moaning in my ear and mumbling how good I felt wrapped around his pipe. Our bodies were drenched with sweat. We both came hard in a matter of seconds. When he made sure that every drop of his nut was inside of me, he rolled over and pulled me with him.

Our chests were going in and out. He rubbed up and down my back. He kissed me on my forehead and told me that he loved me again. I looked up at him and smiled. "I love you, too." I told him and kissed him on his lips.

"You do know now that you know who I am, if you fuck up again, I'm going to kill you." I told him while rubbing on his chest.

"I know baby girl. If you don't kill me, I think our children will come for me first." He said. I didn't doubt that either. Especially Mason. He was a Momma's boy no matter what anyone say. "Can I ask you a question?" Jason asked.

"Shoot," I told him with my eyes closed. I haven't slept in two weeks. I was running on fumes alone.

"Where did the name Gage come from?" He asked me.

I laughed before responding. "When I was young, I killed my Poppa girlfriend. She was so annoying. She used to ask me to get her this and get her that. You know, like I was her personal maid. She asked me to get her something to drink. I went to the kitchen and put rat poison in her tea. She died twenty minutes later. When father found me, he picked me up and brought me to Kymel. He was up in there watching Pet Cemetery. Poppa told him what I did, and he laughed. He told me that I didn't look like the type of person that would kill anyone. He said that my face was to...pretty to be a killer. He was watching the part when the son came back to life and killed the mom. He told me that I reminded him of that baby. So, they started calling me Gage." I replied to him, getting sleepy.

He laughed at my story and kissed me again. "Alright lil Gage go to sleep. We are going to spend the day or two here, and then we are going to see the children." He said. I didn't disagree with him. I closed my eyes and went to sleep his arms.

SIERRA

"You have reached the voicemail box of, 'Brandon'. Please leave a message after the tone. When you are finished with your message press one." I heard the operator say for the tenth time. I had been calling my brothers and father's phone for the past two days now. I knew that they didn't leave without saying anything. And the jet was still at the airstrip. The last time I talked to them, they were on their way to meet up with Jason and his brothers. I tried calling him and his phone kept ringing. I called my oldest brother Leon and left a message on his phone. We weren't that tight like my other brothers because we had different mothers.

I called their phone again and got the same results. "Fuck it," I said. I jumped in my car and went to D1 to confront JJ. I knew he was probably there trying to get into something. It was eleven, so the club was packed. I pulled up on the side of the club and parked. I pulled the side door open and the guard was at the door.

"You can't come through here." He told me.

"What are you talking about? I come through this way all the time." I told him.

"Not no more. You have to enter through the front entrance just like everyone else." He told me and shut the door.

"This is bullshit!" I yelled. I walked around to the front entrance and tried to walk-in. The guy at the door stopped me.

"Hey, get yo ass at the end of the line." He pushed.

"For fucking what. I am here to see Jason. He is going to fuck you up when he finds out how you are treating me." I told him.

"Yeah right. If you were here for Jason, yo ass would have got in through the side door. Take yo ass to the end of the line." He said while letting a few people in. I turned around and saw some of my friends already in line. I walked over to them and started talking.

"Hey girls. They have new guards at the door. They must not know who I am. Y'all mind."

"Girl not at all. Jason is going to be pissed off." Deion said. They were there when Jason approached me in the club. They said that he never done nothing like that. When I got to the front of the line the guard removed the rope and kept his eyes on me.

"Don't start no shit in there." He told me.

I rolled my eyes and kept walking in. Once I got in, I told the girls that I had to use the bathroom. I took a detour and went straight to the office. I was about to knock when I heard someone moaning. I knew this nigga wasn't up in here fucking somebody.

"Bring that ass back Ty. Fuck, I missed this pussy. Yo ass ain't going nowhere." I heard JJ tell someone.

"You talking that big shit. You better make sure that yo ass hold onto me this time. You could see how slippery I can get." The woman told him.

"See, you play too fucking much. I put this on everything. You. Ain't. Going. Nowhere. Test that shit if you want and get yo back blown out." He growled at her. I ain't gon lie and say that I wasn't turned on by their dialogue. The shit had me tightening up my legs.

I shook that shit off and knocked on the door. I was ready to interrupt whatever they were doing. I waited for another minute and started knocking harder this time. The door flew open with a pissed off JJ.

"What the fuck do you want?" He growled out. I ignored him and the sweat that was running down his face.

NEICY P.

"I need to talk to Jason." I told him. He looked at me like I was stupid.

"And," he told me.

"And, I need you to tell me where he is or get him on the phone." I almost yelled.

"Man, get your duck ass away from my shit with all that. I ain't calling my brother away from his family to fuck with you." He said and slammed the door in my face. I heard him talking to someone on the other side of the door. "Come on Tyja, damn." He said. The door opened, and a dark skin chick appeared.

"What do you want with my brother-in-law?" She asked me. I knew this chick wasn't claiming JJ hoe ass. He was with a different girl every night.

"Girl bye. You haven't been fucking JJ long enough to call no one family. He just had another bitch up in here last week. My friend to be exact." I told her.

She laughed and shook her head. "Baby, that was before I came back and locked his ass down. What he did before me, doesn't have anything to do with the here and now. But I see you checking for mine hard and chasing after my sister old man." She beamed.

"I know that you ain't talking about the bitch with the kids." I asked to be sure.

"The one and only." She said with a bigger smile.

"Aye, Tyja stop that shit, bring yo ass back in here so I can break yo back." JJ yelled out.

"Well, gotta go," she said and tried to close the door. I put my hand on it and stopped it from closing. "Girl, don't be one of those pathetic ones that don't know how to let go. Because I could tell you that my sister is not the one to play with. Go ahead and move on, boo." She said.

"Fuck yo sister. When I do see her again, I am going to fuck her up and the stupid ass kids." I screamed in her face. And in no time, I was laying on the floor with the chick standing over me.

"Bitch, you fucking with the wrong one." She yelled. I got up and we started fighting. I pulled on her hair, but she was tagging my face.

The security pulled me away from her and JJ had the woman in his arms.

"Calm yo ass down." He told her.

"Fuck that! That bitch threatened my sister and my God babies." She screamed at him. JJ turned around and faced me with the look of pure hatred. He walked over to me and stared me in my eyes.

"You betta watch what you say, before you end up like your people in the lost and found section." He whispered harshly. I felt my eyes tearing up.

"What did you do?" I sighed out. He gave me a deadly smile and didn't respond to my question. He looked at his security guys and told them to throw me out and never let me back in the club. "Throw her ass out the side door and don't let her ass back in."

"Where is my father and brothers? What did you do to my family?" I yelled all the way to the door. When they tossed me out, I pulled out my phone and called my father's phone again. It went straight to voicemail. I sat on the ground and cried. My brothers and father were dead. I stood on my feet and walked to my car. I sat in my driver's seat contemplating my next move. I was going to call some of my dad's associates to tell them what happened to them. Or, I could call in the Elite assassins to take care of the Davis crew. Yes. I heard that Gage was back and laying muthafuckers out. I was going to pay her two-extra mil for the children.

My phone started ringing and I prayed that it was my brothers calling me back. When I looked at it, I saw that it was Justine, Vince's sister. "Hello," I answered.

"Hey Sierra, are you ok. You don't sound too good." She said.

"No, I'm not. I just found out some sad news." I mumbled.

"Oh, Lord. I'm sorry for whatever you are going through. I am still trying to get over my uncle's death. My mother has been going crazy. Vince been trying to find out who did it, so that he can retaliate with the rest of the other families." She said. And that was my opening. My father told me that Jason and his brothers were at that last meeting.

"Hey, Justine. Did Vince talk to Jason, yet? You know that me and him been fooling around a lot lately and he told me that he was there at the meeting." I said.

"No, but yes. Vince said he talked to Jason, but they were told that the Davis crew weren't there. My brother did find it odd that they weren't, by them being one of the main families in the Stand. Vince called Jordan and Jason told him that it was Leng that sent assassins to kill them. We went over the books and we did see a lot of shit that my uncle was into. Vince tried to set up a meeting with them, but they refused and told us not to contact them no more. Leng told Vince that he lost two good men over the shit."

"I don't understand. With all the firepower that the Stand has, how is it that he only lost two good men." I urged her on.

"I know right. Vince and Dorian, Derrick other son, went over the crime scene photos. None of the shit is adding up. Leng men were killed a mile away from the Center. They also pulled up some of Leng's assassin's work and they all use guns. They weren't as messy as the murders in the Center." She said.

"Damn it," I mumbled.

"What? What is it?" Justine asked.

"The night of the meeting, I went to Jason house and saw the bruises and shit on his body. I didn't think nothing of it until I saw the bloody clothes on the floor. Jason is also good with knives." I whispered.

"Sierra I am going to call you back." She said and hung up. I smirked and drove off from the club. If they don't finish them off, I will be putting in an order for Jason and his little family.

JORDAN

Everything looked like it was going good for the family, for once. Jason and I have our family. JJ was working on one with Tyja. When Jason left to go get Joel, JJ went at Tyja.

"Aye, you and yo girl foul for that shit. How you running around here with one of the deadliest assassins and not let the man you were fucking know what was up?" He drilled her. Tyja looked up at that nigga like he was small. She shut her computer down and turned towards JJ.

"Because, I was only fucking you. My loyalty is to my sister. If she wanted you to know, she would have told you." She said and bumped his shoulder. "Now, if you excuse me, I gotta go see Ma-Ma and my babies."

"Don't be calling my Mommy, yo Ma-Ma. Stay yo lying ass in here and wait to hear word from your Michael Myer's ass sister." JJ told her. Tyja laughed and walked back to get in JJ's face.

"I know you ain't talking, with the Good Son sitting over there." She told him.

I frowned at her and shook my head. "Hell no. I didn't try to kill my brothers." I told her. She looked over at me with dead eyes.

"From the way yo plan went, you could have fooled me." She said and walked out the door. I didn't know how I felt about it. I knew that what I did to my family was fucked up and that I had to endure the digs from everyone. But damn, the Good Son.

JJ turned around with his phone in his hand texting. Tank looked at him and laughed. This nigga's fingers were moving at lightning speed. "Who are you texting, bruh?" He asked him.

"I gotta let these hoes know that I am off the market. I ain't letting her go this time. And if you fuck this up for me again, I will send Madison for you." He said. Anyone would have thought that, that was a good joke. But nobody wanted to see Lil Maddie.

I was chilling with Lilly and JoJo at the park. We tried to get as much time in with him as possible. We knew that Jeremiah was going to take up most of our time. Joel told us that she was going to stay near, just in case JoJo wanted company. Maddie and Mason were already calling our children their brothers. And that shit warmed my heart. This was exactly how we pictured it.

Lily was sitting down reading a book, while I was playing pitch and catch with JoJo. I ain't gon' lie, lil dude had an arm on him to be five. He kept backing up to throw harder. I called him in so that I could give him the talk that Lily been telling me to give him. He ran up to me and looked up at me.

"You tired, Dad." He asked.

"No, I ain't tired. You not doing a lot to make me tired son." I told him.

"Well maybe we should switch it up. When you throw the ball at me, I'll catch it and try to run past you. If I make it to the other end, you have to throw it to me again. But if you get me, I'll toss it to you and you will have to get past me." He said with confidence.

"Alright. Bet. We could do that after I talk to you." We walked over to the blanket where Lily was sitting on. I passed him a Powerade and pulled one out for myself. "You know, when Jeremiah gets here a lot of things are going to change. By Jeremiah being a baby, he is going to need a lot of attention. I don't want you to think that it's because we love him more, because we love you both the same. But if you ever feel that way, let us know. You could talk to us about anything, son. You know that, right?" I asked.

"I know Daddy. You are going to spend a lot of time with Jeremiah, cuz he doesn't know how to do things by himself like me. He is going to need help with everything. But you don't have to worry about that. I got yo back." JoJo told me. I looked over at a smiling Lily. I swear sometimes, I thought that he was here before. He always said the right things, at the right time. He was more ready for Jeremiah than we were. I dapped him off and he went to Lily, to give her a kiss.

"Now that the talk is over with, let's get you tired." He talked that shit. Lily burst out laughing, but it ended in a groan. I looked over at her and she had her eyes closed, breathing heavy. I motioned for the guards to pick our shit up while I got Lily to the car. "Aight, baby. Breathe in and out, sweetie. Just like you are doing." I told her, while I placed her in the car. JoJo got in and put his seatbelt on. When we all were secured in the car, I pulled off and headed to the hospital.

I pressed the speed dial button on my car to call Ma first. She didn't answer. I called Jason next.

"Yo, what's up?" He answered all relaxed and shit.

"Aye, Lily is going into labor. We are on our way to the hospital. Where is Ma?" I asked. You can hear him repeating what I said to the people that were in the room.

"She took the twins to the grocery store. I am gon' call Igor's phone. He is with Ma and the children. We on our way though." He said and hung up. I was driving like a bat out of hell, trying to get Lily to the hospital. My phone started ringing while I pulled up at the hospital. I didn't know the number, so I sent that bitch straight to voicemail. It called me back three times after that. When Lily got in her room and was secured, the same number popped up on my phone. I pulled it out and answer it.

"Who this?" I asked quickly.

"You lied to us nigga." The caller said. I pulled the phone back and looked at the number again. I still didn't recognize it. I put the phone back to my ear.

"Look, bruh. I don't got time for the riddles and shit. Tell me who you are, and we could get the shit over with quick." I sneered at this fool.

"Nah, nigga. We gon' play this game right now. Cuz you see, yo family be all about the games. So, let's play nigga." He yelled out like a hoe. I saw my people running towards me. I told Tyja and T Glenda to go in with Lily. The rest of them held back waiting for other instructions. I put lil stupid ass on speaker.

"Say what you gotta say bruh and get off my phone." I said to him. Tristan jumped on the phone and called Dex to trace the call.

"Oh, you want to know what I got to say, huh. Tell me this, nigga. Guess who I got my eyes on at this moment." He said. Everybody went on alert and started looking around. Joel looked at me and tilted her head. Her eyes got wide, and she took off running. Jason was right behind her, with JJ. "Tell them, don't worry. They ain't gon' make it in time." The nigga said and hung up. I dialed Igor's number and his shit went to voicemail. I called Kymani's phone to see if there were extra guards put on them.

"Yoooo," Mani answered.

"How many guards do you have on the twins?" I rushed and asked him.

"Nine. Why?" He answered with concern.

"Some nigga just called my phone and said he got eyes on them." I told him. Mani hung up the phone. The doctor called me in and told me that Lily was ready to give birth. "FUUUCK!" I yelled out and stormed into the room.

MA-MA

*I*gor just told me that Lily was about to give birth to my other grandbaby. We were already in the check-out line. I paid for the groceries and we headed back to the car. Mason kept looking back for some reason. He did that all in the store. I had my fire on me and was ready to kill a muthafucker if they were looking at them. I didn't play that shit. Damn perverts be trying to kidnap children in stores and on the playground. I knew one thing. If anybody take these two, they are going to wish that they read the fine print, I tell you that.

Once we got to the car, Madison grabbed a bag out of the shopping cart and placed it in the back of the trunk. Igor was helping with it as well. I walked over to Mason and tapped him on the shoulder.

"Boy, what is wrong with you?" I asked him. He acted just like Jason. He looked around and began walking towards his sister.

"Maddie, get in the car. You too, Grandma." He whispered. I looked over at Igor to see if he saw what was going on. He looked around and shook his head. Maddie turned and looked in the same direction that Mason did.

She put the bag back in the shopping cart and got in the car like her brother told her to. I put my hand in my purse to wrap it around my nine. "What you see, baby?"

"It's what I don't see, Grandma. None of our guards are around. Their cars are missing as well." He said right before a bullet hit Igor in the head. I pushed the basket out of the way and grabbed Mason. I opened the passenger's door and pulled him in with me.

"Get in the back and put your seatbelt on. The both of you." I told them. When Mason was in the back seat, I moved over to the driver's seat. I pressed the car to start and put it in reverse and drove off. When we got to the end of the parking lot, a man that I have seen around the children jumped in front of it. He looked like he was shot, from the blood all over his clothes.

He came around and jumped in the passenger side. I peeled off and asked him what happened. "We were in the car, waiting for you guys to come out, when these men came in front of the car and started shooting. I jumped out and started shooting at them. They got me in the shoulder. When they saw that y'all had come out they moved in y'all direction." He said.

I looked over to see his shoulder. It was leaking out so much blood. "Maddie, baby see if you could find something to stop the bleeding." I asked her. I was driving us straight to the hospital. I looked in my rearview mirror to see if someone was following us. It was clear. I looked back and saw that Maddie and Mason were looking at the man in the passenger seat. Mason looked at me and shook his head. He held up the man's phone and enlarged it for me to for me to read it.

V: Bring them to us alive. We are going to take care of them and will pay you when you get here

Well, this lying snake ass bitch. I took a deep breath and remained calm. I didn't know how my babies knew what they knew. But I trusted their instincts. I looked down at my purse and saw that it was between his legs. I looked back at the children. Madison sat back and watched Mason wound her purse strap in her hand.

The guy in the passenger seat started patting his pockets, like he was looking for something. He looked over at me, and Mason came over and wrapped the purse strap around his neck. Mason put his feet on the back of the seat and pulled. The man got wild and started swinging his arms. I was dodging him and the traffic. Mason pulled and pulled 'til the strap popped. The man leaned forward and started wheezing for air. I took him by the dreads and slammed his face on the dashboard.

"Grandma look out!" Madison yelled.

I looked back at the road and saw that I was about to hit a car. I swerved into the other lane and then off the road, to keep me from hitting another car. I pressed on the brakes and came to a hard stop. I tried to take my seat belt off but was stopped by my own gun in my face.

"If you move, you old bitch, I am going to kill you and the children. Get out the car and don't try shit." He said to me.

I got out the car with my grandchildren. They both looked like they were ready to kill this fool. We had to be smart and strike when the time was right. I grabbed and pulled them close to me. A van pulled up and the door opened then three men jumped out with guns. They gestured for us to get in the van. I pushed the children behind me and got into the van with no worries. I knew that my children were coming for us.

They brought us to a big ass lab or facility with four floors. It was wide and surrounded by people. I didn't know if they were preparing for the war that they knew they had started or what. But fucking with my sons and Joel's family, they were going to need a lot more people than the ones they had.. We walked in and there was the Police Chief and Captain waiting. They nodded their head at the asshole that betrayed us. He just didn't know how bad he was going to get it. And for the first time, I was going to sit in when he got tortured.

"Do not hold them. Whatever is the plan, get on with it and move on. There is no need to prolong their deaths, when it's Jason that you really want." Captain Akerman said. He looked over at me and didn't hold my stare. He knew that I recognized him. That was why he wanted us to be killed quickly. Police Chief Bossier looked down at the children and shook his head.

"You all are savages." He said and walked out of the building. The Captain walked out with him with his head down.

They pushed us into the elevator and we went up the fourth floor. I placed my body in front of my babies to shield them from whatever was on the other side of the elevator doors. Mason was having a tough time standing behind me. He kept squeezing my hand. Once the doors opened, the asshole pushed us out and directed us to a room across from the elevators. He opened the door and we walked in, to a room full of people. Mason and Madison came from behind me and held my hands. The wives of the Stand members, were sitting around the table. Derrick's wife Whitney stood and addressed me.

"Hello, Joyce. It has been a long time." She spoke.

"Fuck all the pleasantries if you brought me here to kill me. We didn't get along before and I still don't like you." I told her. The bitch acted too bougie for me. She always thought that shit was too dirty for her. I didn't have time for that. I looked at the other wives and these bitches were weak too. They let their husbands cheat and beat on them. I tried to be sympathetic to their feelings, but you can't feel sorry for stupid people.

"Have you ever wondered why Joyce?" Whitney asked.

"Nope. Haven't lost sleep behind it either." I replied.

"Yeah, you wouldn't. The only lost that you have suffered from was of Senior." She sneered. "Everyone around this table has lost more than you. Our businesses are failing, while yours are booming." She laughed out. "You guys have money coming in from every angle imagined, while some of us have to file for bankruptcy, live with other relatives, or have to find jobs."

"I know you are not up in here complaining about my husband being a man. Or about how my husband raised my sons to be responsible men. Child, bye." I waved her off. "Just because your husbands left everything to the sidepieces and all the other outside kids they have, does not make it right for you to kidnap me and my grandchildren to tell me about it. Girl you could have called me on the phone for this. I wouldn't have answered, but hey, it beats getting killed by my sons."

Julie stood this time, seeing as Whitney wasn't getting nowhere with her interrogation. "All we want to know is, why your son had our sons killed." She asked.

"He had his reasons," I told them. Even if the reasons were fucked up, they'd never know that. We all told him this and moved on from it. I couldn't imagine how she was feeling. Jordan took her only son away from her. No matter the situation, I would never throw some shit like get over it at them. They were hurting and acting out on it. If I had to pay the price for that, oh well, but my grandbabies didn't have anything to do with this.

She held her head down and Janice jumped up and spoke. "And our husbands."

"My children didn't have anything to do with any of your husbands' deaths." I told her.

"That is bullshit. I got information that they were there, and that Jason went home with blood all over him." A young girl intervened. I looked over at her and hunched my shoulders.

"It doesn't matter what my answers are. You are going to think what you want to think. If you have any questions about what has happened to your family members, ask my sons." I told them, finishing the conversation.

"We tried to give you a chance to save you and your grandchildren. But we could see where your sons got their stubbornness from." One of the men stepped forward and said. "Put them in the cage. Set whatever Steel needs to take care of them." He said.

The traitor pointed his gun at me. I turned with my babies and walked out of the room. We got back on the elevator and went to the basement. It was dark and musty. I wanted to reassure my babies but didn't want the asshole to hear me. I squeezed their hands and smiled down at them. They smiled back at me with no worries. They had four steel cages around the room. Tables were lined up around an operating table that had blood and body parts. I turned the twins away. Traitor opened the cage door.

"Get in and don't make a sound." He said. We all walked in and stood in the back. I made the babies face the wall, as I turned towards the room. The cage door closed and he left the room. Men walked in and started cleaning the room.

"How are Nanna's babies? Are you ok?" I asked them.

"We are fine. Are you ok?" Mason asked.

I looked back at them and smiled. "Nanna is good. I'm hoping that they will find us in time." I said.

"They will Nanna. You have your watch on. Daddy and Mommy will come for us." She said. I looked down at the watch and saw that nothing was on the display screen. I pressed the button for it to come on and got nothing. "Son of a bitch." I whispered harshly.

"What's wrong, Nanna?" Mason turned around and said. I stood in front of him to keep him from seeing the body parts.

"The battery died." I told him. Madison turned at that and looked around me. "No Maddie. You don't need to see that." I told her.

"It's ok Nanna. Our Uncles killed the men that was trying to kill us, while we were there. And Uncle Mel sent the video of the people getting killed at the last meeting. We pretty much saw dead people before." She said and moved around me, with Mason following behind her. They started talking to each other and nodded their heads. Madison pulled out a hairpin from her head and passed it to her brother. Mason then walked back towards me and grabbed my hand. "Nanna, just go with it." He whispered and pulled me back.

"Excuse me, Sir. What are you going to do to us?" Madison asked with terror in her small voice.

One of the men stopped and looked at the cage while the others continued working. She batted those pretty brown eyes at him.

"Hey, don't fall for that shit. Her father is Jason." One of the other men spoke.

"Who gives a fuck who her father is? They are still kids, man. I ain't down fa killing kids." He said still looking at Maddie.

"Jacoby, we ain't killing nobody. All we are here to do is clean. You told me that you were down for making some money for your family. Stop being a pussy and get the work done." The guy said. Jacoby looked at me and then back at the kids. He sighed and continued cleaning. Jacoby looked like a kid his self. He was short and skinny with the small dreads in his head. He was midnight black with grey eyes.

"My Daddy have lots of money Mr. Jacoby. If you help us, he will give you and your family whatever you want." Madison told him. He stopped but didn't look up this time. The door opened and in walked a big white man. He was over six feet tall and was pushing two-sixty. He had a bald head and tattoos all over it. I walked forward and pulled Madison back from the cage. The newcomer walked up to the cage and stared at me. He looked me up and down, then shook his head in disgust.

His eyes then landed on Madison. He licked his lips and grabbed his self. Mason pulled her behind him and I jumped in front of him, hitting the cage.

"Look here, you big muthafucker. You will not get your hands on her. I promise you that." I vowed through clenched teeth. He looked at me and smiled with his rotten teeth showing.

"Oh, I will do more than that. That's the least I can do after what yo son did to my family." He tilted his head at me before continuing. "I am going to record it and send it to him. He will have a nice souvenir. Be ready for me when I get back." He said and walked out the door.

Madison came back to the front of the cage and began to talk to Jacoby. "Please Jacoby. Don't let the big man do that to me. Help me." She said with tears in her eyes. The men started packing their things to leave. The boss of the group looked at Jacoby and shook his head.

"Do not get involved, bruh."

"I gotta daughter nigga. We all do. I can't sleep knowing that I could've helped them. Y'all go ahead. I'll take this lick on my own." He said moving towards the cage. The other men walked out the door with their supplies. Jacoby ran towards us with his tools. "I am going to try and get y'all out of here."

"No, we just need your watch and screwdriver." Mason stepped forward and said. Jacoby stared at him with confusion but complied. He handed the watch to Mason. "Nanna, take off your watch." He told me. I pulled my watch off and handed it to him. Mason switched out the batteries and the watch came back on. Mason pressed the button on the side making the watch beep.

"Thank you, Jacoby. Now get out of here." I told him.

"Are you sure? I don't want to leave y'all in here." He said.

"Don't worry, nigga. You about to be in there with them." One of the guards said behind him with a gun pointed to his back.

"Fuck," Jacoby hissed and put his hands up. The guard passed his keys to Jacoby to open the door. Madison grabbed my hand and pulled me from the cage. Mason stood on the side of the door. Jacoby opened the door and pulled it opened. Once he was in, the guard, put his gun away, closed the door, and reached down to get his keys. Mason grabbed the man's hand, pulled it through the cage, and stabbed his wrist with the screwdriver.

"Ahh, fuck," the guard yelled out in pain.

Before he could pull his gun again, I ran to the cage, grabbed the guy's head, and slammed it into the cage. The guard fell with the screwdriver in his wrist. Mason pulled it out and stabbed it in his ear. Madison came forward and kicked the door, which pushed the screwdriver further in. The guard fell to the ground. We got out of the cage and headed to the door with a shocked Jacoby. We didn't get far because the child molester along with some of the men that was in the room was at the door.

The big man tried to grab Madison, but Jacoby jumped in front of her and punched the man in his face.

"Run," Jacoby yelled. The men pulled out their gun and waited for us to make a move. The big man blocked Jacoby's right swing and uppercut him in the stomach. Jacoby went down and threw up all over the floor. The big man started towards us again, but Jacoby grabbed his leg. The big man slammed his feet into Jacoby's face, making his head hit the concrete floor. He was unconscious, and blood was leaking out of his head. "I guess I could start off with him first." He said.

Madison and Mason started talking to each other again. "Hey, shut that shit up and get back in that cage." The man said. He was the same one that sent us down here. Madison's baby eyes wasn't going to work with none of these men. It was my turn to think of something. We were walking back to the cage and crossed over the dead body, while the big man carried Jacoby to his operating table.

"Leave him alone!" Madison yelled.

One of the men pushed her with his gun and Mason lost it. He snatched the screwdriver out of the guard's ear and ran towards the men. The man raised his gun to shoot at Mason. I pushed his arm and the gun went off, shooting the wall. Madison bent over with her hands on her knees. Mason leaped on her back and landed on the man's shoulders. He raised the screwdriver up and stabbed the man on top of his head. The man fell forward. Right before he hit the ground, Mason pulled the screwdriver out of his head and rolled in front of us. Baby boy was ready to protect us with a screwdriver, against men with guns.

"What the fuck?" One of the men yelled. Their faces were something that you could have taken a picture of. He raised his gun, but the leader of the group stopped him. He smiled at us and winked.

"AAHH," Madison yelled. I looked back, and the big man had my baby by the neck. Mason rushed one side and I rushed the other. He raised his arm to block my hit, which left his side open. Mason stabbed him in his side. He dropped Madison and backhanded Mason in the face. My baby went flying to the floor. I pulled the screwdriver out and stabbed the man repeatedly. I pulled it out the third time and tried to stab him in the chest. I didn't move quickly enough, because his big ass fist landed in my face, sending me a couple steps back into the arms of one of the guards.

Madison was sitting by her brother. The guard picked a screaming and kicking Madison up, and placed her back in the cage with me. They put Mason in a cage by his self. "Can you finish the job?" The leader asked.

"This shit ain't nothing but a scratch. Let me clean up and do what I need to do." The big guy said and walked out.

I stood at the front of the cage yelling for my baby. "Mason! Come on, Nanna's baby! Get up!" I yelled. I looked down at Madison and she was staring at the men with her mother's dark eyes now. She pushed her bangs back from the front of her head and glared at them with a menacing look. "What are you looking at?" The leader asked.

"Dead men," she spoke coldly in her accent coming through.

"Little girl please, your father doesn't have enough men to save you from this. He may be good, but he ain't that good." He told her and turned to walk off with the rest of the group.

A vicious smile appeared on her face. "Mi tink dat yuh did a smart man, mista." She told him. "Mi cyaa tell yuh who's inna my fambly tree?" She asked and didn't wait for him to answer. "Well, yuh aready kno mi fada's side. Suh, Mi wi just let yuh kno who pon mi mada's side. First it a fi mi mada Joel. Den mi two uncles Kymel an Kymani. An den there a mi grandfatha, Callum." She said. The whole group turned towards the cage with terror on their face. "What did you say?" One of the other men asked.

"Callum," she repeated. "Mi Papa. Yuh kno him?" She asked incredulously.

"Callum, that is over the Elites." The leader asked.

"Yea, yuh duh kno him. Wow yuh kno dem all." She said with a devious smile.

Another man stepped forward with a question. "Who the fuck is all?" He whispered. You can hear the fear in his voice.

"Well mi uncles are Shadow and Reap. Mi mada is...," she paused and looked at the men on the other side of the cage. The lights began to blink off and on. The men pulled out their weapons readying themselves to shoot. The lights stayed on in one part of the room where Gage stood with her wild hair and dressed in all black with a big ass knife in her hand.

"Gage." She spoke and ran towards the men. The lights were still blinking, but more so with guns firing. You could actually hear the blades swinging and hitting the flesh of the men in the room. They were screaming and begging for forgiveness. This went on for another minute before the lights came back on.

There were bodies everywhere. Some of the men were laying on the floor with their stomachs cut open. It looked like a horror movie in there. The leader was the only one standing in the middle of the bodies. He raised his trembling hands at Joel.

"Hi, Mommy." Madison spoke.

"Hi, Lovey." Gage spoke with her blade pointed towards the ground.

"There is no fucking way that you are Gage." The leader yelled.

Gage smirked at him. Shadow came walking out of the corner on the far end of the room. Reaper came out on the side of our cage and leaned against it. Mind y'all that there were no doors in those areas of the room. The leader started moving the gun between the three of them. The lights went off again right before a shot rang out. The light came back on and the leader was sitting on the floor with no legs, no arms, and no head.

Shadow came and opened our cage, as Gage ran to the cage where Mason was. She shot the lock open and went into the cage. When we were free, we all ran to the cage. Joel was talking, trying to wake Mason up. "Come on, mi Lovey. Talk to Mada." She whispered softly, trying to keep her emotions in check. Mason was bleeding from his nose and ear. The big man did hit my baby hard. I was praying that he didn't do major damage. Mason's head started moving and he began to moan. "Hey, mi baby." Joel said.

"Mommy?" He said in a groggy voice.

"Yes, baby. It's me." she said picking him up and sitting him on her lap.

"I'm ok, Mommy. Stop babying me." He said then wrapped his arms weakly around her. Shadow and Reap began to laugh. Madison walked over to them and laid on her brother's chest.

"I love you, Brother." She told him. He placed his hand on her face and smiled.

"I love you too, Pretty."

JASON

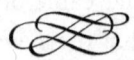

I know y'all are wondering what happened after we ran out of the hospital. Joel got on the phone to track the children's iPad, which they never leave home without. Tyja let us know that they left them at home that time. The rage from the both of our bodies was fuming the air. People that were trying to past us, while we stood at the entrance of the hospital, had to find other ways in.

I called Dex and put him on speaker. "I need you to trace my mother's watch, ASAP." I growled out. He didn't ask any questions. He started typing on his keyboard and said shit. "What?" I said through clenched teeth.

"Nothing is coming up. I think that her watch is dead." He said.

"Did you get anything on trace?" I asked.

"Yes. It was Dorian's number, Derrick's other son." He said. Joel was talking to someone else on her phone and told them about Dorian. "I want you to send me all of the addresses to every business the Stand members own. I also want everyone that is associated with them. Do you understand me?" I told him and hung up.

Joel was still talking on the phone when I got off mine. The look in her eyes was something that I thought I would never see. Worry. She was worried about our children and my mother. To possess the type of skills we have and lose the most important people in our life, was devastating. My heart was hurting knowing that they were in the hands of stupid muthafuckers. Joel turned and faced me when my phone began to ring. "What you got?"

"A lot of their businesses has been going downhill since the death of their husbands. Two of them or going bankrupt and a few of them lost everything. Houses, cars, money, property. Everything. They also had to pull their kids out of college or any other private schooling. That was why Dorian was home." We heard him hit a few more keys, while our patience was purely gone. "I do have something on Derrick's wife Whitney. She's been fucking with the Police Chief. That could be another reason why an Amber Alert hasn't been placed on them. I see that a lot of calls had been made about the incident at the grocery store. But not one cop showed up."

Joel's phone rang and she answered hers. She gestured for me to follow her to the car. I followed and continued listening to Dex. Shadow and Reap pulled up in full gear all ready.

"Kemp Sander's is the man that took them. Pops and Pun is takin out that nigga's family as we speak. The only thing we are waiting on is a location." He growled out. We jumped in the car and went to their house. Joel ran to the basement of the house. JJ and Tank met us at the house with a couple of men with them. I stayed on the phone with Dex until something came up.

"Holy shit, I got it. The watch was just activated back on. They are at the James Hall's facility." Dex shouted through the phone. Joel came up from the basement in all black, ready. I got up and held my hand out.

"Let's go get our babies." I told her. She smiled and grabbed my hand. When we got to the facility we all split up and went in different entrances. JJ and I went through killing everyone we ran into. We got up to the fourth floor and walked in every room. We kicked down one door and saw this big ass white dude. I knew who he was by the tattoos on his head and shirtless back.

"Rusty Connor. They called you in to kill my family." I held the gun on him. He was sporting some deep ass stab wounds.

"Yeah. You know everybody walking around here scared of the Davis crew like y'all unstoppable. Cleary that shit ain't true or your Pops would be here right now." He told me. I knew what he was doing and at this time I didn't care. I still didn't hear anything from Joel about our kids. I was ready to fuck his ass up. I passed JJ my gun and was ready to do just that.

"Aww, Jason. You sure that you don't need a weapon for me." He said cracking his knuckles. "I guess you want me to put my hands on you, like I did your son." This bitch said. I stopped and looked at him. JJ pointed his gun at this nigger.

"Nah fuck that Jason. Let me shoot his ass bruh." He said while stepping forward.

"On everything I love man, if you touched my kids, I will have you begging for death." I told him.

He didn't say anything but stared right back at me. I knew Rusty and his sick ass ways. Him and his family was running all type of illegal shit around the U.S. Me and my Navy crew was given orders to wipe their ass out, but Rusty's punk ass was in jail at the time. I guess he heard what I did to his people. But that shit wasn't going to have nothing on what I do to him.

He kept smiling and started talking again about what he wanted to do with Madison. JJ was yelling for me to take this fool out. I was seeing more than red at that point. I began to walk towards him when the door opened behind us.

"Jason," I heard Joel say. I kept walking over to Rusty, when the sweetest little voice that I ever heard almost brought me to my knees.

"Daddy." Madison called.

I turned around so quick that I almost got dizzy. Ma was standing with a bruised face. Shadow had Madison in his hand. Joel was holding Mason in her arms and I saw blood on his clothes. I looked up at Joel and she nodded.

"He is good baby. Let's go home." She said.

Madison jumped out of her Uncle's arm and ran into my arms. She hugged my neck tight and whispered everything that Rusty did and said in my ear. I kissed baby girl on her forehead and squeezed her tightly.

"It's alright baby. Daddy is going to take care of it." I told her and looked over at JJ. "Give that bitch a sleeping pill. We are about to make a movie." I told him.

"No problem big brother." JJ said and walked over to Rusty.

Rusty tried to swing on him but JJ ducked and hit that bitch with my gun. Rusty's ass dropped flat on his face. "Hey, come get this nigga and carry his ass to the theater." He yelled. Ma walked over to me and gave me hug. JJ was standing next to her and examined her face.

"Damn Ma. Who hit you like that?" He asked.

"That big muthafucker right there. And I don't care what you say, I am going to be right there when you kill his ass. Perverted bitch." She said and walked over to kick him in the face. She turned around with something else to say. "Oh yeah. Joel, tell Tyja that I need some information on the wives of the Stand members. They also had another lil young bitch in here. She had to be related to one of the Stand members. Those bitches were here talking shit. Me and yo T Glenda are going to pay them a nice lil visit." She said.

"The wives were here." JJ asked.

"Yeah, they thought y'all had something to do with their husbands getting killed. The young girl said that they talked to Jo and he said that y'all didn't." She said.

"Yeah Ma. We were there for that phone call. I just got to find out who told them that we did it, to have them coming for us like they did." I said staring at my sleepy baby girl.

"Well, we are not going to find it out today. Let's get home and recap on this shit on tomorrow." Mel said.

Madison's head popped up and looked at me. "Daddy, we gotta help Jacoby." She said.

"Who is that, Lovey?" Joel asked her. Madison told us how he helped us and jumped in for her when Rusty reached out to her. "Aye, get him the best doctors, medicine, and everything else he need. I don't care for the price. Make that happen for me Tank." I asked him.

"I got you, Cousin." Tank said and went out the door with a few more people. After Rusty was loaded, Tank put Jacoby in his car and drove him to the hospital. We got in the car with Shadow and Reap. We rode home together like a family.

"I GOT A SURPRISE FOR YOU, Lil Man." I told him. He was riding in the passenger's seat with me, to a surprise location. We just came from the barber. Lil Man got a nice fade like his Pops. He was sitting there looking just like me. I barely was able to keep my eyes on the road.

"Daddy, please don't take me to Chuck-e-Cheese. Uncle Mel brought me and Maddie there yesterday to play the games. We almost got in trouble when he cursed the woman out, because she was taking all of the pictures with the fake Chucky." He said. Their uncles were always doing shit like that. They would take the children to places that are for kids and have the most fun.

"No, I am not taking you there. I owed something to you and now that you are better, I think it is the best time for you to have it." I told him.

"Cool," he said. He was playing on the watch that we got him and Maddie. They were able to text and do more shit on theirs. Tristan and Dex put all types of games on there for them to play. I pulled my car up in the back where there were other cars parked. I got out and JJ jumped out with me.

"Are you taking me to see a movie, Dad?" He asked surprised.

"What's wrong with the movies?" I asked him, walking in the back door. He shook his head and replied.

"Nothing is wrong. There is not a movie out that I would rather see. But if you want to see something, I am down to watch it with you." He said.

I opened the door to the section where everybody was waiting and pushed Mason in first. He saw his uncles, grandparents, and his mom there. Tank and T Glen was there along with Dex and Jacoby. Jacoby survived his head trauma and was now working in the car dealership with Jordan and JJ. I also gave him a mil for saving my daughter. Jacoby moved his family out of that beat-up neighborhood and placed his daughter Allure in a private school.

They were all sitting in the front row, waiting for the curtains to go up. Mason moved to greet everyone. When he was done, I called him to the front of the stage. "I know that we didn't talk about what happened in the room with yo sister and Grandma. Madison told me what happened and what the man had said. We also know that you were protecting yo sister and, if you didn't, Lord knows what would have happened. But because of your swift thinking, you saved her life. I didn't know what to give you to show you how much I appreciate you for doing that, even if it is your job."

He looked up at me with pride in his eyes. "Thanks Dad." He said.

"Don't thank me yet." I told him and pressed the button for the curtains to go up.

Rusty was strapped to the operating table, ready to get operated on. Mason walked forward and looked down at Rusty. As tempting as it was, no one touched him while he was here. I had men watching over him. More so, I needed them to keep our brothers away. JJ already tried to get in there with Jo to beat on him. The men called me and told me that Shadow and Reap appeared in the building without setting off any alarms. When I told them my plans, they agreed and made me promise to let them watch.

Everyone pulled out their popcorn and candy, waiting for Mason to perform. I knew the shit was sick on our part. We can easily try to lead him in another direction. We did give him options that he and his sister refused. This was the life they wanted. And when the time came for them to not want it anymore, I'll be there to support them in that as well.

Mason turned around and gave me a smile that resembled my own. "Yuh di best Fada." He said to me.

I went to the rack on the side of the wall and pulled an operating coat off. I ordered that and a lot of other things when I found out about them. I held it out for him to put it on. I buttoned it up and took a step back. "Do you want me to stay up here with you, Son?" I couldn't help asking.

He answered me with his back turned. "No, Fada. Yuh hav seat wit da rest."

I looked at Joel and she smiled back at me. I jumped down from the stage and took the seat next to her. Mason picked up the scalpel and started making small deep cuts all over Rusty's body. His screams were muffled from the tape that was on his mouth. Mason pulled the tape off his mouth. "Mi wa fi hear yuh scream."

"Fuck you! I am going to kill you and your whole family, you little piss ant." Rusty told Mason. Mason went back to the table and grabbed some pliers. He shoved it in his mouth, not too gently and clamped it on his tongue. He pulled his tongue out his mouth and sliced it off.

"Ahh!" Rusty started screaming.

"Dats betta." Mason whispered.

He opened him up and began to pull out each organ out of his body, naming them as he went. No one was able to wipe the proud look off my face. My son was a true Davis and Bailey. A deadly combination. We all sat there enjoying the show, when Joel's phone began to ring.

"Aye, lil simple ass girl, did you read the sign that said turn off all cell phones before stepping into the theater." Mel told her.

She turned around and glared at him. "Sit back with yo hot ass breath." She told him and answered her phone. She listened and waited for the person on the other line to finish talking before hanging up. "Yo girlfriend put a hit out on us. I guess it's time for me to pay her a visit." She whispered to me.

"I am coming with you." I told her with no room to argue.

"That is fine." She said. "Are you sure that you could watch me kill your lil girlfriend?"

"You are going to make me fuck you up." I leaned into her.

"Mm, you know I like that rough play." She said and placed her lips on mine. I sucked in her bottom lip and bit it tenderly. She moaned in my mouth and grabbed my face, to pull me closer.

"Say bruh, why don't y'all go sit in the back with all that shit." Mel told us and dumped the whole box of popcorn on our heads. He got up and went on the other side of the theater.

Rusty's screams brought our attention back to the stage. Mason had a hammer slamming them into his ribs. Blood was splattering everywhere. The men cheered him on like his ass was playing football. Mason finished hacking his ass up with no remorse. When he was done, he received a standing ovation. My son bowed his head. He took the jacket off and placed it in the bin. I was going to burn them tonight. Mason turned, jumped off the stage, and ran towards us. I caught him just in time, as he leaped into my arms with the boyish smile.

"How did I do, Dad? Mom. Did I make you guys proud?" He asked.

"You sure did, Son. You made us both proud." I told him. "I gotta take you home and get you cleaned up. Then me and you could do whatever you want." I told him.

"Can I go and talk to everyone else first?" He asked. Once I placed him on his feet, he took off running towards his Uncles. JJ was dapping him off and told him how cold his moves were. Shadow and Reaper stood back with a smile. I looked around the room and realized how crazy we really were. Ma and T Glen waved everyone off. They already took care of the wives and Vincent sister. We found out that she got information from Sierra. I almost forgot how Ma and T Glen were back in the day.

Not only were the wives taken care of, but the Chief of Police and the Captain was dealt with in a gruesome way, by Callum. He skinned their ass alive and left them both bleeding out. That worked for us in more ways than one. That left two spots opened to be replaced by two cops that are on our payroll. They didn't have nothing major to do. We never called our cops in for nothing. They were there "just in case" shit happens.

"When are you going to take care of Sierra and Kemp Sanders?" I told her.

We let Kemp get away on purpose. We were trying to see who he was going to run to after everything was over. And in no time, our techs tracked him down. He had been shacked up with Sierra now. He been so deep in her pussy that he didn't bother checking on his family. The Punisher took out his whole family at once. When everything was going down, his family was having a family reunion. Punisher poisoned all the food that they had. They all were dead in a matter of minutes.

"Shadow wanted to kill Kemp himself. Since he hired him to watch over the children, he felt that it was his fault." She told me. Mason ran over to us with a big smile on his face.

"Dad, is it ok if I go with Uncle Jo. I want to see JoJo and Jeremiah." He asked. I looked over at Jo and he nodded his head.

"That is cool with me Lil Man, just be good. Aunt Lilly still needs her rest."

"That is why I am going over there. I am going to help Uncle Jo and JoJo take care of the baby." He said. He gave us both a hug and ran back to Jo. They waved us off and left as well. Jacoby came and dapped me off. "Hey, I ain't never seen no shit like that. You got some ruthless ass children." He said.

"I know. That's great, right." I told him.

He shook his head and laughed. "I guess. I'll see y'all tomorrow." He said and left. Dex, Tristan, and Tank walked over to us with JJ. "What y'all about to get into tonight." JJ asked.

"Well, I got info on Sierra and Kemp. I am going to change and go take care of that right quick." Joel said.

"Do you know where they are?" Dex asked.

"Not yet. I gotta get with Tyja for that info. I know that they are still in town." She replied.

Dex shook his head and held his hand out. "I could do it for you. Pass me your phone." She gave him the phone and he began working on it. He passed it back and there was a Satellite picture of the house that Sierra and Kemp were in.

"How the fuck did you do that?" Tank asked while looking down at the phone in Joel's hand.

"It was something that the three of us was working on. I'll tell y'all more about it later. I got a date tonight. Catch y'all later." He said and walked off.

"We are about to hit the club. I gotta go and pick up Tyja first. I'll meet the rest of you there." JJ said and left with the rest of them. We walked over to the other group. Shadow and Reaper were talking about going back to the island with her Parrain and father.

"So, what do you want me to do about Kemp?"

Shadow's eyes widened at the question. "It's a go?" He asked.

"Yeah, I am about to pick up a few things and head over there. You down." I asked him.

"Fucking right." He said. Joel went and hug her father. We were going to go down there next week. He wanted to spend more time with her and make sure that she never fall off again.

We all said our goodbyes to each other and left to go back to the house. Joel was sitting in the passenger's seat texting someone.

"Who are you texting like that?" I asked her.

"Someone you love." She answered. We got to the house and grabbed our things. "We are going to meet Shadow there." She said. We jumped back in the car and went to the house that Sierra and Kemp was held up in. I parked in front of the house and jumped out. Joel got out with her hair pulled up. It confused the shit out of me, because she didn't look like she was ready to kill anyone. "You ready." She asked me.

"Are you?" I asked, confused.

"Yeah, I am ready. Let's go through the back door." She said and walked quietly to the back. I followed behind her watching the way her body looked in that leather. It had me ready to throw her ass on the side of that house. "Just think, the sooner the better." She said, without turning around.

"That's you with all the bullshit. You don't look like you ready to kill anyone." I told her. She walked in the back door without answering me. We heard Kemp's ass moaning throughout the house. We walked upstairs and went into the room that the noise was coming from. Joel opened the door, and I went in behind her. Sierra was kneeling in between Kemp's knees with his dick in her mouth. Joel looked at me and smirked.

"And you wondered why I never kissed you." I said out loud for them to hear me. Sierra jumped up and turned towards us. Kemp tried to roll over to his gun that was sitting on the nightstand but was stopped by the knife that Joel threw at him.

"I don't think so." She said.

She walked over to his pants that was on the floor and threw them at him. "Put some clothes on." She told him. Sierra didn't have to be told. She reached out for her robe when she saw that it was me at the door.

"What are you doing here?" She asked.

"Let's not play stupid. You told the Vince sister that I killed their fathers. Them muthafuckers kidnapped my children, with that bitch help." I said pointing over to Kemp. "They were going to kill them and my Mom for what, because you and I are not together." I said calmly.

"Really nigga. You think this is about you and me." She yelled. "This is about my brothers and my father. You killed them. It was only right to take from you the way that you been taking from everyone else."

"I told you not to send yo punk ass brothers my way with all that bullshit. I warned you and you didn't listen. You are the reason that they are dead." I told her flat-out. I could hear Joel's feet tapping on the floor, bored with our conversation. I looked back at her and she was staring at me.

"Are you done?" She asked with an attitude.

"You and that fucking mouth." I told her and took a step back. This was her show. I came with her to watch her in action.

"You not going to have to worry about that mouth for long. Gage is coming for you and yo kids." She spat at me.

Kemp was smiling at that. What was so funny about all of this? Kemp didn't know that he was hired to watch Gage's children. He was never around the children when it was time for them to train. Joel didn't trust no one but the guards that her father hired from the island. She said that people from here could have been bought easily. She wasn't lying about that.

"Well, that won't be happening, Sierra. You see, the information you and your family got about me on the internet, was what I wanted you to see. If you would have known who I really was, you would have left me and our children alone." She said, walking towards the window and looked out of it.

"I remember when I was younger, just starting out in the game. I was just finishing up with a job, when one of the men yelled that they were going to kill my father. The fury I felt was unbelievable. Like I said, I was young and couldn't control those emotions then. I found myself losing it and doing the unthinkable to that man. I drained his blood, along with his family and bathed in it. That was my first time losing control." She said.

Joel turned and faced us again. She began to walk over to Sierra. Sierra was looking at me and Kemp. She was scared after hearing how someone died threatening Joel's father. Sierra knew that it was going to be worst for her threatening her children.

"I understand how you felt when Jason and his brothers killed your family. This was your way of acting out like me. You didn't have the particular skill set, so you hired someone to take care of it for you. Totally understandable. Right. Is that what you were feeling?" She asked her.

Sierra looked at her and nodded her head. Joel stood in front of her and tilted her head. "That is good. I may not understand what it feels like to lose my father, but the thought of it drove me mad. Just like the thought of Jason being taken away from this family infuriated our sweet little girl." Joel said.

I turned around and saw Madison walking in with Shadow behind her. The pigtails that held her wild hair was loose and all over her face. She had on all black leather outfit with some black Timberlands. Her eyes were just as dead as her mother's got. Madison was holding the knife that I bought her in her left hand.

Joel took a step to the side and let Sierra see why the room got quiet. Sierra's eye went on Madison and she gasped. "What the fuck is going on?"

"We talked about this already, Sierra. You told me that you understood. I understood it as well. Now you gotta know that if you are living, our daughter is going to worry about her father's safety. She doesn't want to do that, right Lovey."

"Right Mada." Madison said and started walking towards Sierra.

Sierra grabbed the lamp by the bed and threw it at Madison. Madison slid on the floor and dodged the flying lamp. Kemp tried to jump out of the window. Shadow didn't want to miss Madison's kill. He pulled out his gun and shot Kemp in the back of his head. Shadow pulled a chair from the desk in the room and sat down.

Sierra reached back and grabbed the knife that Joel threw at her. She swung it at Madison, almost catching her in the face. When she swung it the third time, Madison grabbed her wrist and pressed on it.

"Oh shit," she yelled out holding her wrist. She tried to kick Madison in the face. She ducked and stabbed her in the back of her knee.

"Fuuck! Help me! Someone, please help me." She started yelling holding her knee. Madison looked down at her and watched as she cried out. I thought that she was going to walk away and let her live. She stared down at her for five minutes straight. Joel watched with Shadow, waiting for her next move. Quickly and with a growl, Madison stabbed Sierra in the chest.

Shadow looked disappointed at the kill and got up from his seat. Madison looked back at smiled at us, right before pressing the button on the knife. Sierra's upper body exploded. Madison's head dropped back and enjoyed the kill.

"Oh, that was some tight shit. Fuck you, Joel. Maddie is my favorite now." Shadow yelled. "I got the best niece and nephew in the entire world." He said. Madison got up and passed me her knife. She was quiet and looked pissed off.

"What's wrong baby girl?" I asked her.

"Nothing," she said and walked past me to pick up her book sack.

She went into the bathroom and closed the door. I looked back at an amused Joel.

"What is wrong with her?"

"She didn't think that it was going to be that messy. She is taking a shower." Joel said. My phone started ringing while we waited for baby girl to get out of the shower. I pulled it out and saw that it was Mason. "Everything good, Lil Man." I asked him.

"Yeah everything is good. Is Madison ok? I felt something strange and wanted to know if she felt it too." He asked. Madison came out of the bathroom with her clothes in a trash bag that her uncle passed her. She passed it to Shadow and came towards me with her hands up. She had on her pajamas. I picked her up and passed her the phone.

"I'm on my way to you. We can talk about it when I get there." She told him and hung the phone up.

"How are you feeling, Lovey?" Joel asked. Madison looked back at her with tiring eyes.

"I'm okay Mommy. When Uncle Mel came and got me, I was sleep." She said.

"Ok, Pretty. You had us worried there for a minute. I thought that you were going to change your mind." I told her.

"It wasn't that. I was thinking of torturing her but went ahead and got everything over with quickly." She said and laid back on my shoulder.

"Aye, I can bring her over to Jordan house if y'all want." Mel suggested.

"Is that ok with you, Lovey." Joel asked.

"Yeah that is fine." She said and reached out to Mel. I kissed her on the forehead and squeezed her tightly. He came and grabbed her out of my hands. Something in me didn't want to let her go. I wanted to bring her home with me. Especially after what Joel said to Sierra. I didn't want my baby to think that I was going anywhere. Joel stood on her toes and whispered something in her ear. Madison laughed at her mother and wrapped her arms around her.

"Not today." She told her. We all walked out as the clean-up crew was walking in.

"The night is young Mrs. Davis. What would you like to do?" I asked Joel as we walked towards the car.

"Let's talk about this Mrs. Davis shit. I don't remember me agreeing to no such thing." She chuckled.

"I don't find nothing funny about that. Yo ass is going to be agreeing to a lot tonight." I grabbed her around her waist and brought her body close to me.

"So, you say, Mr. Davis." She said and pulled me down to her lips.

DEX

I was just getting in from another date with a chick I met up with online. It was going well, until she started talking about her baby daddy issues. Don't get me wrong. I didn't mind being with a woman that had children, but it was clear that she was still having feelings for her. He was blowing up her phone the entire time she was with me. The date I had last week, after Mason's kill didn't go well either. She smoked cigarettes and that was a turn-off for me.

I got in my house and threw my keys on the table. I went to the kitchen to get me a bottle of water before I showered and went to bed. My watch beeped twice when I got into the kitchen. That was strange. My alarm was detecting more than one person in my house. Tristan and Tyja was out at the club with everyone else. I looked down at my watch and saw that the person was downstairs in my lab.

I backtracked my steps and went downstairs with my gun in my hand. I wasn't worried about them getting into my system; my shit was always locked and secured. When I got to the bottom step, I saw a man standing in front of my blank screens. I lifted my gun up and walked towards him.

"Can I help you with something?"

"Put the gun down, Dex. We all know that, that is not in your

DNA. All this shit right here is what you know." He said and turned around. I didn't lower my gun because the muthafucker that was before me had been missing. He took out his whole crew in the jungle. I didn't know how this nigga mind was set up at that moment.

"What are you doing here, unannounced?" I asked instead.

He put his hands up and backed up. "I didn't come here for any trouble. I just need your help with something. I got a call some weeks back about my father. I tried to find him, but somebody killed him. I knew that the shit was going to happen one day. I'm not worried about him that much. But, I am worried about my brothers and sister. She called me to let me know that my brothers were with our Dad at some meeting. I tried looking into it some more but kept hitting a brick wall. I tried calling my sister again, but I can't get an answer. I don't know if the same people that took my brothers and father out, took my sister out. If I give you a name, do you think that you can look into it for me?" He asked.

I looked at him to make sure he was telling the truth. We all were taught to hide our emotions in the Navy. Jason, Sincere, and Matthews was the best at it. You could never tell when they were happy, sad, or angry. The way that Matthews was displaying his feelings, showed me that he was telling the truth.

"Leave me the name and I'll get you the information that you need in a day." I told him. He went into his pocket and pulled out a folded piece of paper. He reached over my computer and placed it on my desk.

"Good looking bruh. Next time I'll knock." He told me and walked up the stairs. I followed him and made sure he left. I put on my secondary alarm system and went back downstairs. I didn't know who fucked with this man's family, but they were about to get dealt with. I sat down at my computer and grabbed the folded paper. When I opened it, I dropped it back down like it bit me. I picked up my phone and made the call that was about to change everything.

"What's up Dex?" Jason answered.

"We got a serious problem." I told him, while loading up my computer. I could hear him getting up on the other end. "What is it?"

"When I got here, Matthews was here waiting for me." I told him.

"What the fuck did he want?" He asked, as a door slammed.

"He wanted me to find his sister and his brothers." I told him and pulled up the cameras that were around my house. They were all disconnected. I tried to pull up the other cameras across the street from my house and saw that it was surrounded by men and Matthews.

"Ok, and what." He asked.

"Don't come here, Jason. He got my house surrounded. I will call you with another location." I told him.

"Wait Dex, who are his brothers and sister?" He asked.

"Alan and Brandon were his brothers. And Sierra was his sister." I told him right before my house blew up.

To be continued....

SUBSCRIBE

Text Shan to 22828 to stay up to date with new releases, sneak peeks, contest, and more...

WANT TO BE A PART OF SHAN PRESENTS?

To submit your manuscript to Shan Presents, please send the first three chapters and synopsis to submissions@shanpresents.com